STASI VICE

 Stasi Vice is also available
as an audiobook

Also by Max Hertzberg

The East Berlin Series
Stealing The Future (2015)
Thoughts Are Free (2016)
Spectre At The Feast (2017)

Reim Series
Stasi Vice (2018)
Operation Oskar (2019)
Berlin Centre (Bruno Affair 1) (2019)
Baltic Approach (Bruno Affair 2) (2020)
Rostock Connection (Bruno Affair 3) (2021)

Other Fiction
Cold Island (2018)

Non-fiction
with Seeds For Change
How To Set Up A Workers' Co-op (2012)
A Consensus Handbook (2013)

After the experience of the East German political upheaval in 1989/90 Max Hertzberg became a Stasi files researcher. Since then he has also been a book seller and a social change trainer and facilitator.

Visit the author's website for background information on the GDR, and guides to walking tours around the East Berlin in which many of his books are set.

www.maxhertzberg.co.uk

Stasi Vice

Max Hertzberg

P 4 5 6 7 8 9 10

Published in 2018 by Max Hertzberg
www.maxhertzberg.co.uk

c/o Wolf Press, 22 Hartley Crescent, LS6 2LL

A CIP record for this title is available from the British Library
ISBN: 9780993324796 (paperback), 9780993324789 (epub)

Set in 11 on 12½pt Linux Libertine O

SEPTEMBER 1983

1
KÖNIGS WUSTERHAUSEN

It was meant to be a simple job. Lean on a few people, get them to shut up. Intimidate neighbours, bribe officials, appeal to the socialist conscience of Party members.

But clearing up after the boss is never a simple job. Not that I'd ever say so in any official way. But this is just between you and me, and I know I can trust you, don't I?

And what are bosses for if not to create work? The boss in question has a fine life. A villa in the *Botanik*. Every morning he gets picked up in a company car and brought to work. Every morning he leaves his fine family behind, two kids, one of each. Blonde hair and blue eyes, you know the kind. Every morning, they stand at the garden gate with the blonde-haired-blue-eyed *Mutti* and wave their starched white handkerchiefs. Good-bye *Papi,* as he goes off to secure the socialist future.

Doesn't matter how early I arrive, he'll be behind his desk, checking his watch and flicking specks of nothing off his uniform sleeve.

Prussian bastard.

I hear you, exactly the kind of bloke who's going to play away from home. And not for BFC Dynamo. Play away-games and sooner or later things will get messy, you can bet your wages on that.

And so I ended up playing cleaning-lady for the Boss.

★

I entered the *Konsum* department store at half-past nine. That was my first mistake, right there. I was busy congratulating myself on my timing, the queue of pensioners looking for rarities that might have been delivered by mistake had cleared off and the store was fairly empty. Instead of being smug I should have used my nouse and hightailed it back to the capital for a quick look in the registry.

First rule of any operation: check the files.

Normally, before any operational measures begin, a file is opened. Then you make cross-references and end up with more lists, keys, indexes and summaries than are in the Berlin telephone book.

Normally.

Problem was, this wasn't normal. This was my boss telling me to sort out his mess on the sly, and *dalli dalli*. If I checked the files back at the Centre my search would be logged, and then all you need is some busybody wondering why a grunt from Main Department VI is looking at the files of nobodies from a sandy town on the edge of Berlin. That would have landed me in the shit, and not just with the Boss.

So I didn't look through the files. Didn't check whether anyone on my list was known to the Ministry in any capacity, shape or form. Or any other ministry for that matter. Any Party members with connections in the right places? Any family members or close acquaintances higher up the pecking order than the Boss? Any cross-links, existing files, references or indexes on any of them?

If I'd had time to go through the registry at my own pace and in my own way, I would have spotted the connections immediately. That would have saved me a good few millimetres of shoe leather and a truck-load of hassle.

Enough with moaning into my beer. I was telling you about this little operational measure on the side. There I was, standing on the ground floor of the *Konsum* in Königs Wusterhausen—to call the three tiny floors of this provincial shop a department store stretched my imagination too far—and demanding an audience with Citizen Dittmann. No need to show them the detective's disc, they made me for the member of the state organs that I was. They ushered me into a poky storeroom with no natural light.

And there she was, my first operational target. Petite, greying hair tucked under a dark blue paisley headscarf, fingers bent with rheumatism. But her arthritic fingers weren't stopping her from skimming the consumer goods, taking little cartons of sewing supplies out of the packing cases and putting them in a cardboard box to be handed out to friends later. She was so busy she didn't even notice me.

"Needle and thread in short supply again?" I enquired, friendly enough. I find it easier to play good cop, at least until the need arises. Then I'm happy to show my true colours as bastard cop.

Dittmann nearly jumped out of her skin. While she made a show of wringing her hands she was nudging the box of illicit wares further under the counter.

I flapped the tin disc at her. Just like her colleagues on the shop floor, there was no real need to get the piece of metal out, she already had me pegged. But a little bit of psychological reinforcement goes a long way.

"Can I help?" She was being polite, wondering whether I'd noticed her little game.

"Paragraph 173, section 2 of the criminal code. Hoarding of goods," I helped her out.

"Is that why you're here?" She sank into a chair. A

3

handkerchief appeared and she mopped her soft face.

Obviously it wasn't why I was here, they'd have sent a bull to lift her for that, if they'd bother at all. But I left her hanging—I'd helped her enough already.

I asked to see her *Ausweis* and in return pulled out a mugshot of the Boss's pretty lady and held it under Dittmann's nose. "Know her?"

Dittmann peered at the picture. It was black and white, but you could see the fine featured woman was a blonde, her eyes blue—just the way the Boss liked them. I watched as Dittmann poked around in the pocket of her pinny until she found her glasses. She perched them on the end of her nose then tilted her head so they wouldn't get in the way of the photograph she was looking at. People do the stupidest things, but I've learnt not to rub their noses in it, not when I want something from them.

"Frau Hofmann!" Dittmann seemed pleased to place the face, maybe she thought if she got full marks I'd let her off.

"See her much?"

"Regular customer, always very polite. Saw her just last week-"

"See her outside of work?"

"Oh." Dittmann slid her glasses up her nose and looked at me. The lens distorted her eyes, making them bulbous and shiny. "Not in any kind of trouble, is she?"

"It is your duty to answer my questions." The cold stare always does it.

"Walking in the Tiergarten park last week, perhaps it was the week before. With a gentleman-"

"This one?" Another mugshot for her to peer at, this time of the Boss. How could he be so sloppy, taking his lass for a hike round the local beauty spot?

"Quite rude, I greeted them as they went past and if

4

looks could kill-"

"This concerns the interests of society." I took the photographs back. "Not to mention your own."

Dittmann took her glasses off and gave me a blank look.

"Citizen Hofmann is of operational interest. Therefore, for political-operational reasons you may not mention to any person that you have seen Citizen Hofmann in the presence of this person, nor that you and I have ever met. Failure to comply would indicate a negative attitude towards our socialist state. Is that clear?"

Dittmann looked unsure, so I gave her another nudge.

"Paragraph 173, section 2," I said.

I got my notebook out as I left the Konsum and crossed Dittmann off the list. One down, three to go. At this rate I'd have my Boss's mess sorted by the end of tomorrow. Day after at the latest.

2
ZERNSDORF

You might think my day got off to a bad start when the Boss sent me down to the end of the S-Bahn line to sort out his mess. Actually it didn't. Give me a choice between pushing paper round the desk all day or keeping my hand in the business of giving folks a hard time, well, I'll let you work out which one I get up in the morning for.

When the single carriage train wheezed into Zernsdorf station and I found out I still had a kilometre to hike, that wasn't a disappointment either. Sure, it didn't make me smile, might have made me wish I'd brought a company car. But what really wiped the grin off my sweaty face was when I rocked up at the People's Own Works Liqueur Factory Zernsdorf and found out that the nearest liqueur was in a grocery store back in the centre of Königs Wusterhausen. The rattle of crates of lemonade and table water empties being thrown around the yard was the soundtrack to the shakes I was beginning to get.

"So why is it called a liqueur factory if all you have is limo and Club Cola?"

I was so distracted by the lack of serious alcohol that I let the porter enter my details into the log book, but soon came to my senses and snatched my clapperboard out of her hands before she could get to my roll number. It wasn't a problem, I'd flashed her one of a small selection of official passes I carry around for the purpose. This one matched the tin disc, today I was a detective in the People's Police.

Over at the lorry park a crew of overalls was loading up a flat-bed W50 truck with wooden crates. They took one look at me and the Party badge on my lapel and decided to put their backs into shifting them crates round.

"Marco Westhäuser?" I called out.

A fat guy grunted and poked his thumb at the third truck along, the one that was as dirty as washing hanging on the line in Bitterfeld.

I wiped the licence plate and wrote down the number, kicked the tires a bit and dusted off the toecaps of my boots. No crew in sight, probably in the works canteen loading up on beer and poppy-seed cake. I pulled open the door and put one foot on the wheel to haul myself into the high cab. It stank of sweat and brown-coal dust, so I left the door open while I made myself comfortable in the co-driver's seat. First thing I looked at was the manifest, neatly attached to a clipboard. There was my guy's name on the lading bill, along with that of his workmate.

"Oi! What you doing in my lorry?" It wasn't a question, not coming from the brick shit-house steaming towards me. It was a demand backed up by implicit threats.

I stayed in the cab, it gave me the advantage of height if he decided to kick off. I got the disc out and waved it in his face.

"K," I said. That one letter is enough, short for *Kriminalpolizei*. Always makes people stop. While he was digesting that, I waved the clipboard at him.

"Leaving paperwork in an unattended cab? Serious."

The brick shit-house shrank back down to human size and his fists unrolled into hands the same size as the mirrors on his lorry. I decided it was safe enough to leave the cab door open. I told the guy to flash me his works pass. Westhäuser, Marco. It was my man.

"Where's your mate?"

"Canteen." Westhäuser hooked a thumb over his shoulder.

Stocking up on beer and poppy-seed cake, just like I said.

"Right, Citizen Westhäuser. You and me are going to have a chat. Get up in the driver's seat." I watched him swing up into the cab with practised ease, then told him to give me the keys.

Before I let myself relax, I gave Westhäuser the up and down, checking for signs of aggression. He was pinned behind a driving wheel the size of the kind of cake a Bigwig would organise for his daughter's wedding. We also had the hump of the engine between us, so I considered myself safe enough.

"This your neighbour?" I asked, poking the mugshot of Hofmann at him.

"Hot lady." He made to take the photo, his lips pursed into a kiss.

"Maybe. You know the bimbo or not?"

Westhäuser put his hands back where they belonged and nodded.

"Seen her around lately?"

"Sure. She lives in the house opposite. Never miss wash day, see her in the garden, hanging out her panties."

Classy. But now down to business. "Enough of the dirty talk already. You seen her with anyone else. A man?"

"Of course. Her and the old man put their best threads on for church. Every Sunday. Stockings-"

I didn't need to hear about her Sunday stockings, so I waved a hand in his face. Shut it.

"What about away from home. Ever bumped into her?"

"Nope."

"Think about it."

So Westhäuser thought about it. I could see the thoughts passing through like those toy trains the Pioneer kids run round that loop in the Wuhlheide park.

"Nope," was all he came up with after he'd let the thoughts go round a few more times.

His trains weren't on the fast track, which gave me a bit of a problem. The Boss's orders were to find this guy and turn him off. His crime? He'd clocked the Boss and his girlfriend on a romantic day out at a nearby lake. The Boss had probably been looking forward to a bit of groping in the undergrowth that day, but the girlfriend had other ideas. She'd insisted on going shopping in the village *Kaufhalle*, just in case they had anything she couldn't get here in Zernsdorf or in Königs Wusterhausen. But as soon as they rocked up at the shop, her next door neighbour comes along with a wagon-load of drinks.

Question: was Westhäuser so slow on the uptake that he hadn't noticed his hot neighbour queueing up for a shopping trolley? Or had he just forgotten? If he'd not noticed then the last the thing I wanted to do was to plant the idea that he might have seen her. But if he'd just forgotten there was a danger he might remember again later.

"You deliver to Wolzig?" I asked him.

"Twice a week, Wednesday and Friday," he replied. "Kablow, Bindow, Friedersdorf, Wolzig, Blossin ..." he recited the route plan, quick as you like.

"What about last Wednesday?"

That had him thinking. He started counting on his fingers, then looked up, his face bright and proud. "Day off."

Turns out his workmate and another colleague did the run that day. This easy job was already starting to turn into something messy. No surprises there. In my line of work, you try to clean up the mess left behind by a superior officer then you've got to be prepared to deal with an even bigger mess. Shit flows downwards and outwards, as we say in the trade.

I noted down the names of his co-driver and the colleague who'd stood in that day, then moseyed on over to the administration building. I flashed my K disc, told them to bring me the rosters for the last two months and to show me to the room where they kept the cadre files. The secretary had to break the wax seal on the door to the archive, and once the opening had been documented I booted him out.

I checked through the rosters until I found last week's. There they were, Route B, heading through the eastern edges of KW county, fourth stop: Wolzig.

Westhäuser wasn't on the list for that day.

The names of the two men who had worked the route tallied with those Westhäuser had given me, so I copied out their home addresses and went and got a local map from the secretary. Neither of the men lived anywhere near the Boss's girl, no obvious reason they'd know her.

I put the cadre files back on their shelves and took the sheaf of rosters back to the secretary.

"Thanks," I threw over my shoulder as I left.

"No problem. You're the second person this week who's wanted to have a look."

I didn't react, just kept on walking until I got to the railway station.

3
KÖNIGS WUSTERHAUSEN

My next stop was back in KW, as the locals call Königs Wusterhausen. Having a chat with the local goons was my fig leaf for coming all this way. Or as the Boss would have it: operational conspiration by means of receiving operational reports on the political-operational situation in KW county. Right now, the local Stasi would be bricking it, wondering why an officer from the capital was swinging by at short notice. They'd be checking files, trying to guess exactly which fuck-up had attracted the attention of Berlin. They weren't to know that my job was actually to keep an eye on Western tourists, and there was little call for me to be here. Far as I was concerned, any tourist that made it to this sand pit deserved anything they got from the locals.

After my warm up with Citizens Dittmann and Westhäuser I was in the mood to put some unnecessary heat on the local comrades at the County Office. I flashed my MfS card at the uniform behind the glass and was on my way to the stairs when she piped up.

"Message for you, Comrade Second Lieutenant." She handed over a flimsy.

I gave the message the once over on my way up the stairs, then turned round and headed for the train station. Playing with the comrades would have to wait.

The S-Bahn got crowded as we headed into Berlin, but nobody sat next to me. The citizens of this Republic recognise us trench coats a mile off. They smell the stink that comes off us.

I got off at Schöneweide and hiked to the Clubhouse. Most people are surprised when they hear that we don't have luxury offices at Berlin Centre in Lichtenberg, but here we are, along with a couple of other departments, in a network of sooty-bricked buildings, built as square and regular as a barracks and sandwiched between Schnellerstrasse and the river. I call it the Clubhouse, because I like to think we have a bit more independence, out here in Treptow.

I showed the guard my clapperboard. I do it every day, and every day he examines my pass as if he's never seen it or me before. Finally he saluted and let me in through the gate, and I went to find the Officer of the Day, wanting to know what was so big that I had to be pulled off doing the Boss's graft. Turns out we're a goon short at the Palasthotel in the centre of town. So that was me along with my wee bottle of schnapps doing grunt work the whole afternoon, listening to microphones and watching video cameras of Westerners fucking.

Taking notes, photographs and video footage for *Kompromat* files is slow, boring work. You've seen it once, you've seen it a million times. Captains of industry and greedy politicians come over from the West, keen to make deals and bolster reputations. Nine times out of ten they allow themselves to be dragged into the sack by one of the more willing members (mostly female, but we had a few boys in the mix, too) of our workers' and peasants' state.

4

ZERNSDORF

It could have been the bottle of schnapps I had last night. But ask me, I'll tell you it was the grunt work yesterday afternoon that made my brain jingle. Whatever the cause was, I only started thinking about the Boss's little operation on the way back to Königs Wusterhausen the next morning.

I'd reported for duty in the Boss's office, dead on 7 o'clock, and he'd sent me straight out the door again, all the way down the S-Bahn tracks to KW. He wasn't interested in hearing my carefully prepared speech on why I thought my time could be better spent on officially sanctioned operations. It's not that I didn't have sympathy for the Boss—he'd seen the opportunity for a little fun and he'd grabbed it with both hands. The Firm frowns on extra-marital relations, so the Boss should have been a bit more careful about things, but at least he was trying to sort that out before it was too late.

Still, not my job. After all, he's the one having fun, so how come I end up picking up the tab? Don't get me wrong, yesterday had been fun, but I had other work to do and would have preferred to spend my day in the office.

But when it comes from above, no means no, and I had to give up trying to get out of doing the Boss's dirty work and instead concentrated on an attempt to persuade him to let me make his dirty work as pleasant and efficient as possible.

"I can cover more ground if I take a vehicle," I suggested. "Could be useful if I need to engage in operational observation."

"Out of the question," he snapped.

We both knew the reasoning. If I took my own vehicle an over-zealous official might clock the Berlin plates and make enquiries. I couldn't borrow a car from the transport pool because then times and mileage would be indelibly noted in the Firm's records. That's how it is when you're doing work off the books, you end up spending hours on clapped out S-Bahn trains.

For want of anything else to do on the long, rattly journey through the suburbs of Berlin I put my brain into gear and gave it a thrashing.

Question: if Westhäuser wasn't working last Wednesday, how could he have seen the Boss and Frau Hofmann?

Answer: he didn't. Obviously.

Possible solution number one: the Boss and his girl weren't in Wolzig last Wednesday. They got their days mixed up. After all, I had seen, black on white, that Westhäuser wasn't working last Wednesday.

Problem with solution number one: the Boss was pretty damn sure his day out with the fluff was Wednesday last. When I'd made my verbal report he'd looked doubtful for a moment. He checked his desk calendar (which, in accordance with the paranoid regulations of our Ministry wasn't on his desk, but locked in a drawer). Then with a voice that was meant to discourage me from questioning his memory, the Boss repeated that it was last Wednesday.

That put me in a bind. I had to choose between the Boss's version and the records that said Westhäuser hadn't worked that day.

When I hauled open the doors of the S-Bahn and dropped onto the platform at KW, the railbus to Zernsdorf was on the platform opposite. It was making sounds like it wanted to leave so I crossed over and climbed into the little red pig-taxi. The diesel engine chugged and the doors scraped and squealed until the driver reckoned they were shut enough. Two stops later I was in Zernsdorf.

When I got to the Liqueur-Factory-That-Was-Only-A-Bottling-Plant I stood on the road outside, watching the trucks buzz in and out of the gates like May bugs with serious digestive problems. After a while the porter came to tell me to find somewhere else to enjoy the view, but when she made me from yesterday she stopped and climbed back in her cabin.

Smart lass, she'd go far.

I was pretty sure Westhäuser wasn't lying. For my money's worth, he didn't have enough upstairs to keep a lie going. But I wasn't going to question the Boss's memory either. That way lay pain and misery.

Which meant my only option was to keep working on Westhäuser.

Loose ends. Any investigator hates loose ends, and right now I had one long enough to hang myself by the neck. I didn't want to go through that gate and corner Westhäuser, not unless and until I found out he had actually been working that day—no point drawing even more attention to the Boss and his piece of skirt.

I'd brought a map with me this time, and I checked Westhäuser's address. His street started about a kilometre away, and itself was nearly a kilometre long. Cursing the Boss for not letting me bring a wagon, I hoofed it back along the road.

Zernsdorf was as nice as you could hope for. Lots of small

houses in big gardens; zucchini, tomatoes and pumpkins sprouting wherever you looked. Leafy. Idyllic. Bucolic. All those green-tinged words were why we Berliners had a name for the towns and villages surrounding the city: the *Botanik*. I could see why the Boss liked living out of town.

When I got to Westhäuser's address I felt more at home. A five-storey slab concrete block of flats. Smaller and tidier than the one I live in, but definitely more my style. Woods at the back, the usual Zernsdorf-style small houses and big gardens opposite. One of them must belong to the Hofmanns, but the Boss hadn't given me the address. Wouldn't take me five minutes to find out.

I started on the top floor of the flats, flashing my dodgy tin disc at door after door. Investigating a series of break-ins, did anyone see anything last Wednesday? Know anyone who was at home and might have seen anything? Most of the people living in this block were workers— either at work or night shifters pissed off at being woken up in the middle of the day. The nosy pensioners and interfering *Hausfrauen*, bread and butter to us professional snoopers, were conspicuous by their absence. This was going to take longer than I thought.

Resigned but not discouraged, I started on the well-kept detached homes opposite, deliberately leaving out the house with 'Hofmann' helpfully painted in large white letters on a scabby piece of wood attached to the mesh fence.

My luck changed two houses further on, and not in the way I'd been hoping. I rang the bell next to the garden gate, and a diminutive old biddy humpled down the path, peering at me from beneath a headscarf.

"Is this about Herr Hofmann?" she asked when I flashed the piece of tin.

"What about him?"

She perked up at that, lifting her head and unfolding her back long enough to make eye contact. "Missing since Saturday. Poor Frau Hofmann is in a right state."

I let her ramble on, it's surprising what useful titbits can be sieved out of the verbal effluent of gossips, but I'd already found a nugget of gold, even if I hadn't been panning for it in the first place.

In my world there was only one way to go missing, and that was if and when my Firm decided to do it for you.

5

KÖNIGS WUSTERHAUSEN

It takes years to make a Stasi man. The grooming starts a long time before you've ever had the thought that being an officer in the Ministry would be a fine thing. Like everything else with the Firm, it starts with the files. What are the family like? What about school friends, family friends, activities in the youth movement, grades? They like kids whose parents are in the Party, it gives them a head start in the file department. First thing you know about it is when they're putting you under pressure to sign up to the army for longer than you'd like to, and bang, you're in the Felix Dzerzhinski Guards Regiment. Or on the border. They'll read the files a bit more, watch your progress, and if they like the cut of you they'll take things a bit further. Some casual spying on colleagues, pledge your allegiance and go back to school. All to create the ultimate committed, non-thinking operative.

I blame the Ministry. It failed me. Because it wasn't even midday and here I was. Thinking.

This morning the Boss repeated his order to operationally manage his list of potential witnesses. So what did I do? Only went and found out that the jane's husband has gone missing, and she's well cut up about it. Did I suspect the Boss? Bet your Party card on it.

Right about now would be a good time to check those damn files. Was Herr Hofmann the subject of any operational procedures that could explain his disappearance? If I went back to Berlin and started poking around in the Central Biographical Database, word would pretty soon get back to the Boss and I'd spend the rest of my career steaming open envelopes. Time to call in some favours. But first, seeing as I was down here already, I'd fit in a few more visits to those witnesses.

On my way back to KW, planning my approach to the next name on my list, it struck me that I talked to myself too much. All this jawjaw about thinking had made me clean forget the appointment at 1400 for operational reporting on operationally relevant material obtained during the course of yesterday's grunt work. There'd been a senior Bavarian politician on the other end of my cameras, and I'd been ordered to attend Berlin Centre so the bigwigs could have a look at what kind of fish they'd caught.

It takes nearly an hour and two changes to get from KW to Lichtenberg, and it's times like this that I'm glad I'm not based at the Centre. As it was, providing the S-Bahn didn't break down on the way, I should have enough time to blag a place at a typewriter to write up a report. With luck I could get in and out of the conference without ever being alone with the Boss.

The information exchange went well, the *Bonzen* were pleased with yesterday's catch. Not that they said anything that could be interpreted as encouraging, but they didn't slap me round the chops either. Which kind of proves my point.

I was about to shuffle off when the Boss ordered me to wait outside until they'd finished.

When the Boss's bosses filed out ninety minutes later, cheeks red with drink, he fetched me into the office he'd borrowed.

"What have you got for me, Comrade Second Lieutenant Reim?" He was slumped in his chair. A snapshot of General Mielke looked over his shoulder. It was one of those pictures with eyes that follow you round. For all I knew there was a camera behind it that did follow you round.

"Permission to report on information gained beyond the parameters of the operational plan, Comrade Major?"

The Boss nodded slightly, or it could be his chin was settling on his chest because he needed a nap after all the cognac.

"Comrade Major, information provided by source Westhäuser did not correspond with that in the operational plan. I therefore began an analysis of the source's movements and during the execution of this analysis it came to my attention that Citizen Hofmann, spouse of the lady-"

"I damn well know who Hofmann is," said the Boss, his chin still sunk in his chest.

"Citizen Hofmann is reported to have been missing since approximately 1100 last Saturday-"

"Comrade!" The Boss was on his feet now, fists on either side of the blotter, face hovering thirty-seven centimetres above a gold-plated desk lighter personally presented by Minister Mielke to the usual occupant of the office. "Did I or did I not give you an operational plan?"

"Comrade Major, the operational situation demanded a revision of tactics in order to realise the political-operational aims-"

If the overuse of the word *operational* bothers you half as much as it does me then you'd do well to stay away from the Ministry. No need for me to tell you that, anyone with half a brain cell knows it's best to avoid the Firm anyway, but I'm part of it now, and it bugs me to say the O word ten times in every sentence. I figured this wasn't the best time to submit my concerns about my Operational overdose, not when the Boss was bawling me out.

If it had been an official operation he would have reported me. Then again, if it had been an official operation there wouldn't have been such a problem if operational-tactics had to be revised.

As it was, I was dismissed from his presence, and ordered to continue through the list of witnesses.

6

BERLIN LICHTENBERG

While I was at the Centre I decided to go and see an old friend from Main Department XX, State Organisations, Church and Oppositionals, which always struck me as a strange mix. When I checked his office he wasn't home, but I tracked him down to Building 18, where he was sitting in the canteen. Before I went to his table I had a quick gander at what was being served. I took the rice pudding—the only edible thing on offer.

"Holger, you still owe me?" I asked as I sat down.

"Last time I checked, you were in my debt." Holger was poking a plate of cold roulade and congealed sauerkraut.

"I need a look-see at some files."

He didn't ask me why I needed a look, nor why I couldn't just go to the reading room and check them out myself. "What's in it for me?" He smeared some mustard over the stiff cabbage.

"I'll eat that dinner for you."

"Done." With one hand Holger pushed his plate towards me and with the other he grabbed my bowl of rice pudding.

There was a preliminary file open for Frau Hofmann, the kind that led to an approach. Or, in everyday language: information was being collected with the intention of recruiting her as an informer. The last entry was from two months ago, about the time my Boss had started the affair with her. Handy, don't you think? Oh, and you won't be surprised if I told you which section opened the prelim file: my very own HA VI.

In contrast, Herr Hofmann was a clean slate. There were no operational procedures open against him, nor had there been at any time. The only thing I could find on him were his national service records. Ancient history, not worth blowing the dust off. That meant Hofmann probably wasn't at this moment chained up in Hohenschönhausen, which left only two other options.

Option One: he'd found out about his wife's affair and hot footed it rather than face up to the Boss. If that were the case I could find him within twenty-four hours. Forty-eight tops. Then again, if I went into full-on search mode I'd blow my little side-operation wide open, and the Boss would not be chuffed.

Option Two: the Boss had disappeared him. And I didn't rate my chances of tracking Hofmann down if that were the case.

I didn't like Option Two because it raised the question of why the Boss would want to do away with Hofmann. I don't like questions like that, they're bad for my health.

Since Holger was in the registry anyway, I asked him to pull the files on all the other people on my list. The biddy in the *Konsum* department store was as clean and as dull as a worn whistle. The only reason we had a file on her at all was because of her ex-son-in-law. Dittmann's daughter had been married to some intellectual, but they separated and she took the kids when he put in an application for a one-way exit visa. No bearing on this case, so I left Dittmann and her relatives in the file and turned to Westhäuser.

The lorry driver had an entry, but only because some

overzealous prick had reported him for an off-tone joke at the expense of the General-Secretary of the Socialist Unity Party. Other than that, the sap had let himself get signed up for three years in the military where he spent most of the time in the workshop throwing spanners at tank engines.

The next person on my list was Dieter Berg, and he looked way more interesting. You could tell because his file came with its own trolley. Just like Dittmann's son-in law, Berg had applied for an exit visa. Seemed it was catching, this urge to leave our well-managed paradise of Real Existing Socialism.

I made a note to check whether Dittmann's son-in-law, Heiko Müller knew this Berg and whether he was still in the country or whether we'd let him out yet. Then I carried on reading Berg's files.

We had him on a piece of string and we pulled him into the county offices of the Ministry like a yo-yo. For variety he probably got to see the inside of the County Police Station on a regular basis, too. Usual stuff. Endless interrogations, map out personal connections, dust him down and send him off until the next time. Engineer by trade, now working as a binman. You got to see the world from a different perspective in a job like that.

Finally, we had Heidemarie Müller who worked on the switchboard at KIM, the combine that ran the chicken factory farms and slaughterhouses. She was a candidate for Party membership—a right goody-two-shoes with a repulsively unblemished trajectory through the youth organisations. After a while I couldn't read any more, it was giving me dyspepsia.

Back in Treptow, I had a look at my notes of what the Boss had told me about Berg the Binman. He'd given me a day and time when Berg might have witnessed some knudling: last Friday evening, the night before Hofmann went missing.

I checked my watch—I could still fit Berg in before close of play. I swapped my uniform for a dull brown suit and headed out of Berlin.

Destination: Königs Wusterhausen. Again.

7

KÖNIGS WUSTERHAUSEN

I was already bored of the journey to KW. Knackered workers filled the carriage, their hang-dog jowls leaning on battered briefcases used to carry snap boxes. I only had my thoughts to occupy me since political-operational secrecy demanded that all notes be kept under lock and key back at the Clubhouse. The notebook in my pocket was empty, all used pages removed and filed at regular intervals during operational procedures. That meant I had only my memory to go on when preparing how to deal with Berg.

He would be used to pressure, I thought. Threats wouldn't touch him—when he made the decision to apply for an exit visa he'd already decided he was prepared to lose his job, go to prison and put up with constant hassle by state organs. That meant he wouldn't be a push-over like Frau Dittmann. I didn't have much to offer him other than physical violence, but this wasn't that kind of operation. My only option was to play very-nice-cop. I could put in a good word for him with the colleagues at the Centre, maybe we could look into expedited processing of his application to leave. All lies, but when you're desperate you grasp at straws. And I'm talking about Berg doing the grasping, not me. Not just yet.

Once off the train, I headed to the town's maintenance depot. Bin lorries passed me on the road, kicking sand and dust in my face. When I got there I flashed the tin disc at the porter—my K identification was getting a lot of use these last few days—and wandered around the car park.

It didn't take long. I had memorised Berg's registration number, but the white ribbon tied to the Trabant's aerial made it easy to find. Berg had kept it nice, this ribbon. Symbol of those who wanted to leave the country. It was still clean, not at all tatty. He must have replaced it regularly to keep it looking like that.

I leant against his plastic car and patiently puffed on a cigarette.

There were four dog ends at my feet by the time he turned up. Slightly stooped, dark hair under a cap and stinking of coal ash and rotten cabbage. He took one look at me and the Party button on my lapel, and made for the car door, key held between nicotine-yellowed fingers. I slid along the wing until my bottom was resting against the door so he couldn't open it.

"Not in a rush, are we?" I asked.

"I haven't got time for this." He was considering his options, but like me, he didn't have a whole lot of them.

"You get into trouble because of this?" I pulled the white ribbon off the aerial and twined it around my fingers.

"I know the score." He dropped his bag on the ground, but his keys were still in his hand, ready for use.

"Just thought I could help, that's all." That threw him off balance. He stopped staring at the lock on the door handle and shifted his gaze to me. "Seems stupid to hassle people for tying a bit of ribbon to their cars." I handed him the piece of cloth.

He held it in his hand for a moment before stuffing it in his pocket. "What do you want?"

I looked around the car park, fringed by dusty forest,

W50 trucks thundering in and out. "I could do with a lift to the train station." I moved away from the car, giving him an escape route if he wanted one.

Berg opened the door, threw his bag on the back seat then climbed in, leaning over to unlatch the passenger door. That was all the invitation I was going to get, and it was all I needed.

It's not that far to the station, and when we got there I told him to park the car and switch off the engine.

"You're not from the local police station?" he asked.

"Berlin." I told him. "We've heard stories. Not best pleased."

That confused him again. He looked at me with wide eyes.

"Seems the colleagues down here might be getting a little enthusiastic about dealing with citizens who don't want to be citizens any longer." I offered him a cigarette. He took it, but didn't light up.

"It's the same everywhere," he said after a while.

"So you don't want to make a complaint against the behaviour of my colleagues?"

He shook his head, no. He'd be a fool to make a complaint, and everyone in the car knew it.

"Nevertheless, I have my orders. Tomorrow I begin an investigation into the tactics used by the People's Police County Station here in Königs Wusterhausen." I waited for Berg to take this in. He was probably wondering why I was telling him all this, and I could see his hairline bulge as his brain tried to process what was happening.

"There's one thing you can help me with," I said. "I'm a bit stuck on ascertaining the facts of a case."

"I'm sure I won't be able to help."

"Let me tell you what it's about before you clam up.

Last Friday, after work."

Berg jumped out of the car, then leaned back in. "You got a light?"

I got out and walked around the stern, meeting him on his side. An S-Bahn had just pulled in and a murmuration of citizens was making its way past us. "Last Friday," I prompted as I sparked him up.

Berg took a deep puff then shook his head while exhaling.

"You sure about that?"

But Berg wasn't interested in answering. He'd smoked his cigarette down to the filter, and was watching the clock set into the cross-gable above the station entrance.

It didn't take an officer of the law to work out that Berg was spooked, and that it wasn't the right time to push it. Let him stew for a day or two.

I stuck another smoke in his overalls pocket and headed for the platforms.

8

BERLIN FRIEDRICHSHAIN

When I got home the Boss was waiting for me. I don't mean sitting in his car outside or politely hanging around in the doorway, I mean he was spread out in my armchair, puffing on the cigar I'd put aside for my birthday and nipping on a bottle of heavy Bulgarian wine that my wife had left behind. At times like that, I'm glad I live alone—nobody around to see me looking scared.

"Not a team player, are you Reim?" the Boss rasped between blowing smoke rings.

I stayed in the doorway, ready to make a quick escape.

"What did I tell you? Put your feelers on those people and make sure they stay quiet. Was that not simple enough for you? Did I not explain the operational plan clearly enough? Because I don't remember ordering you to go knocking on every door in Zernsdorf. Nor do I remember telling you to go burrowing through the archives." He was still in the armchair, boots up on the footstool, bullet head on the antimacassar. He wasn't looking at me and didn't see the surprise flicker across my face. He must have had a watch tag on those files, how else would he have found out so soon that I'd had a quiet peek?

There was silence for a smoke-ring or two. He never wanted answers to any of the questions he asked and I'd learned not to offer any.

"Give me your notebook," he ordered.

I took the notebook out of my pocket and brought it over. If he wanted a reason to put me on notice he'd have to find another—my notebook was as clean as a virgin's.

The Boss must have worked that out from the way I moved because he didn't even take the notebook off me, just gave me a look out of the corner of his eye. Blue it was, surrounded by eggy sclera shot through with conjunctivitis.

"Siddown!"

I sat down on a hard chair near the dining table. Out of range.

"You and me, we've got problems. My problem? It's sitting right here in this room with me, and it's called Reim. Way it's meant to work: I give the orders, you follow them. But you're not following them and that's giving me a headache." Smoke ring, appreciative twist of the cigar. "I'll tell you about your problem, Reim. Your problem is that you've got a much a bigger problem than I have. Sure, this operation is off the books, potentially embarrassing for me. But don't kid yourself, if this goes the wrong way, you'll be the one who's neck-deep, not me."

He waited until he'd got a *Jawohl* Comrade Major, then flapped his hand like a seal that's eaten all the fish. Danger over, at ease, Reim.

"You're one of my best operatives, Comrade Reim, that's why I entrusted you with this little operation. But every so often you go off the rails, which makes me think I need to keep a closer eye on you."

I didn't answer.

"Now," The Boss put his hands back on the chair, head back on the antimacassar, cigar back in his gob. "Tell me what you've got."

"Comrade Major-" I began, but he did the seal thing again.

"I said it was off the books, didn't I? We can be casual, call me Fröhlich."

Fröhlich, meaning jolly, was the name they passed down from father to son in his family, but I couldn't imagine anyone could both be related to him and *fröhlich* in any way. Just didn't suit whatever genes gave him fists as big as those chickens they had at KIM.

"Yes, Comrade Fröhlich," I said, trying out the casual form of address he'd requested. "In the course of an operational interview with Dieter Berg, the source refused to confirm or deny that he had witnessed either yourself or Citizen Sylvie Hofmann on Friday last. My operational analysis is that the source withheld information."

"Your operational analysis was that he was withholding information?" the Boss repeated, laughing so much he farted. Just as suddenly as he had started, he stopped. The fart hung around longer than his humour.

"So get it out of him—make it official if you have to! He's a white-ribbon traitor, that's enough to put him in the pen." He mimed dialling a number "Hello, is that Hohenschönhausen Remand Prison? Someone here looking for a five star hotel, do you have a room for him?"

I could have given him my analysis of the political-operational situation, that Berg needed the soft touch and a bit of time, but what was the point?

"Yes, Comrade Fröhlich."

9
BERLIN ALT-TREPTOW

As soon as the Boss decided he wouldn't outstay his welcome, I grabbed the car keys and jumped in my Trabi. I didn't go far, just over the river and into Alt-Treptow. Task for the night: operational observation of Dieter Berg. His file had told me he took part in the regular meets in the Treptow parish church for those wanting to leave our Socialist paradise. I didn't want to get too close, the church is on a very short street and you could bet your bottom Mark that the colleagues from Main Department XX would be there, too. Keen to keep a low profile, I parked on Kiefholzstrasse, around the corner from the church. The angle was a bit awkward, I couldn't accurately identify individuals arriving or leaving, but that was fine. If Berg was there (and I'd arrived too late to see him or any of the other exiteers go in) then when it came to chucking-out time he had only three options: walk to the S-Bahn station for the train home; get a lift home; or go to a bar with others. Options 1 and 2 would bring him straight past me, and I'd be sure to clock either his mush or the Potsdam district D-reg plates of the car. Option 3, the bar, might take him in either direction, but at least I'd see if a knot of people moved off together and I could continue the observation on foot.

It was that time of year when the days are warm, but the evenings get cool. Stationary observation is as boring as watching bluebottles trapped in a jam jar, and when it's cold, it's a mug's game. That was me, comrade. A first class mug and I had a medal I kept in a yellow plastic box in a locked drawer to prove it.

This was a bad place to hang out. Even if that church wasn't one of the main joints for all the malcontents in this part of Berlin, this little corner of the capital had the Wall on two sides of it, and the barracks of Border Regiment 33 on the third side. Wherever you parked you'd be near enough to a restricted zone to read the *Verboten* signs. So it was no surprise when a uniformed cop came strolling down the road on the lookout for anything out of key. I kept him in the mirror and watched his comedy double-take when he spotted me. He straightened his back and pulled his uniform jacket over his belly. Must have made his evening when he clocked me behind the wheel of a stationary vehicle, bottle of beer at my lips. He came alongside, but before he could bend down to do that stiff little salute through the window I had my clapperboard up against the glass. This time I used my real ID: Ministry for State Security. I didn't bother opening it up, just let the flatfoot see the cover— that would be enough, and with a bit of luck he wouldn't log the encounter.

He plodded on without looking back, but did an extra careful job of checking coal-hole hatches and shining his torch along the embankment of the goods railway line that led to West Berlin. I shifted my eyeballs to the church down the side road. I lit another cigarette and waited.

It was getting late when they tumbled down the steps, shaking hands and sharing last words before heading home. A few of them started walking my way, and as they came closer I spotted my mark, Berg, chatting with another leaver. When they got to the Lada that I'd pegged as official they put more effort into their bonhomie, laughing extra loud, making deliberately effusive gestures. But I noticed that once the small group had gone past, a few of them looked over their shoulders, nervous that the goons from Department XX might decide to get out of their car and engage in more than operational observation.

They passed me on the other side of the road, and when they reached the junction with Elsenstrasse I tossed my dog end out of the window, wound up the Trabi engine and jerked it into gear.

I rabbit hopped along behind them, waited in the shadow of the railway bridge, then parked for a few minutes to let them get ahead. It's almost impossible to tail someone on foot with only one vehicle, but fortunately nobody in the group was paying attention, or if they were, they probably thought I was engaged in overt observation. The thought probably pleased them—leavers do this masochistic dance, attracting the state organs' attentions, hoping for a bit of repression and trying to piss us off so much that we give up and throw them out the country. One of those white ribbon guys was probably mentally marking up his score sheet right now: operational tactical observation, ten points. Dream on, buddy, you'll need a few thousand points before we even begin to take proper notice of you.

I parked the car next to the delivery gate of the Electrical Appliance Works on Hoffmannstrasse, opposite Treptower Park S-Bahn station. The works' security guard marched out of his little office, ready to give me grief, but he stopped in his tracks and made a tactical retreat when I got out of the vehicle. Didn't even have to flash the clapperboard at him. I ran across the wide road and into the tunnel to the platforms. Berg's mates were on the up platform, while he was on the other platform, waiting for a train to KW. There were very few passengers at this time of night, so it was easy to spot him, even though he was in the shadows that clung to the old chestnut tree at the far end of the platform. I went up and offered him a coffin nail.

"You following me?" he asked as I gave him a light.

I got my own f6 lit up and drew on it before nodding.

He put that away without response, too busy gulping in smoke.

"You look hungry," I told him.

"No smoking in the church, and anyway, I finished my pack."

I offered him my deck and tossed in the matches for free. He palmed them and chained another butt off the one still in his gob.

"So what do you want?" he asked when he had enough air to talk.

"Friday night. You were going to tell me what you saw."

"Was I?"

A train whined into the other platform. When it clattered out of the station and over the river, Berg's leaver chums had gone. On our platform the indicator rolodexed through destinations until it settled on Grünau.

"You getting this one or waiting for a direct train?" I asked, sick of the silence.

The chestnut tree rustled its leaves. Berg got my pack of f6 out and thought about smoking another one. He put it back in his pocket and spat out the dead end that was still in his mouth.

I looked at my watch, looked at the tree, conkers ripe enough for falling. Wrapped my coat tighter against the gale coming off the river.

Berg was having difficulty getting his next cigarette lit,

but succeeded in the end. He took this one easy, alternating air with smoke.

"Come on, Berg. I'll give you a lift."

I walked off, hoping he'd follow. It wasn't until I'd reached the top of the steps down into the tunnel that I heard his shoes clicking over the granite setts of the platform.

This time of night, the roads are clear and my plastmobil was faster than the S-Bahn, but only because we had a head start. I begged a smoke off Berg, feeling stupid that I'd given him the whole pack.

"You've got to give me something." I told him once we'd got past the complicated bit where the road wants to push you onto the motorway feeder. We stayed on the trunk road, I wanted to avoid all the cameras near Schönefeld motorway interchange.

"What do you want?" he asked after he'd thought about my demand for a puff or two.

"Tell me what you saw last Friday."

"Nothing." His answer came back without a beat's hesitation.

"Sure about that? Yesterday you weren't so sure."

"I'm sure."

"Whatever it is you're scared of, I can help."

Berg took the last ciggie out of the pack and put it in his gob.

I thought about pulling over and chucking him out, but I remembered the analysis my boss hadn't wanted to hear: two pairs of velvet gloves.

We carried on down the F179 in silence, the constant hiccuping of the wheels on the joints in the concrete making me bad tempered. As we got closer to KW, I asked him the best way to his joint and he gave me directions. Other than that he didn't lose another word the whole way home.

I dropped him off at one of those cute little cottages that seem to be a speciality round here.

"Nice place for a binman," I said, trying for small talk.

He didn't bother responding. He unlocked his garden gate and went up the path.

I twisted the gear stick round and let the clutch out, not sure whether I was more pissed off about the wasted packet of cigarettes or the wasted evening.

10
KÖNIGS WUSTERHAUSEN

Top of my list the next morning was to deal with all those loose ends that were so obstinately refusing to get tied. I got off the bus at the bridge over the River Dahme. The bus belched off, and I walked back along the road until the trees of the Tierpark surrounded me. I stood at the side of the main road which ran through the middle of the woods and breathed in the heavy fumes of the sooty trucks and buses. I watched the traffic and checked my watch: thirty to forty vehicles per minute. Double that at rush hour, I estimated, halve it after six pm. From eight o'clock take it slowly down until it's only one or two every ten minutes in the late evening. The Boss told me that Berg had seen the lovebirds on Friday after work. Berg wasn't prepared to talk to me about it, so I had to do my own thinking.

The Boss mentioned Berg and only Berg as witness last Friday. Was that because it was so late in the evening and no other vehicles passed them? Or was Berg the only person that had been recognised? Or the only registration plate that the Boss had noted?

What was Berg too scared to tell me about? Had he associated whatever happened last Friday with the Stasi, and he thought me a cop, lower down the pecking order and therefore unable to do anything about it? Or had he already been threatened? If so, why did the Boss send me after him to threaten him some more? One thing I knew from personal experience, the Boss is quite capable of being threatening and doesn't need any help in that department.

Something happened here in the Tiergarten last Friday, something so big that Berg wouldn't tell me what it was. The very next day, Hofmann's husband had gone missing. Did they connect?

I dropped my cigarette on the forest floor and started walking back to the bus stop.

Right next to the bus stop was a telephone box. Berg the binman hadn't been willing to talk, but when I phoned them up, his workplace were happy to oblige. Berg was on the late shift last Friday, had clocked off shortly after eleven pm. I reckoned he would have got to the Tiergarten somewhere between ten past and twenty past. Road would be pretty quiet by that time of night, so Berg as only witness was plausible.

I stopped thinking about Berg when the bus swayed around the corner. I bought a ticket to Zernsdorf, I still had the mess around Westhäuser to clear up: had he or had he not been working the day the Boss and Sylvie Hofmann went on a jolly to Lake Wolzig?

11

ZERNSDORF

The gatekeeper at the Liqueur factory in Zernsdorf didn't ask to see my disc this time, she let me pass with a dry nod. Westhäuser's lorry wasn't in the loading area, nor was it parked up with the others, so I assumed he was out on a run and went to check out the canteen instead. It was mid-morning, and lunch was being served for the early shift. A quick glance at the *Wurstgulasch* and green beans spread over the compartmented plastic trays told me I wasn't hungry. Nevertheless, the place was full, and I wandered over to the drivers' table.

Conversation stilled as I walked through the canteen, starting up again behind me in a shifting pattern of silence. Same thing happened with the drivers, they got shy when I arrived and stayed shtum when I didn't move on. A few eyed me belligerently, others suddenly found their goulash fascinating. With this kind of effect the detective's disc could stay in my jacket pocket; my face was ID enough.

"Who was working a week ago Wednesday?" I demanded of the silent drivers.

First of all there was no reaction. I lit up a nail and waited, puffing smoke over their food.

Then one of them spoke, and with that, murmurs rippled round the table. Bashful hands were raised, fingers were pointed.

"Any of you see Westhäuser that day?" I asked.

Shakes of heads, thoughtful looks, questioning of neighbours. General consensus: no.

"Willi stood in for him last week—that was Wednesday." A wiry man with thinning hair stood up.

"Who are you?" I moved closer, making sure I was well within his personal space.

"Union rep." He pushed a little blue membership booklet at me, but I waved it away.

"Can we talk?" It wasn't a question, I had him by the elbow and was steering him out of the canteen.

I found a quiet corner in the yard and started interrogating him.

"What kind of worker is Marco Westhäuser?"

"Conscientious enough. Found his level, if you know what I mean."

"I don't. Talk straight."

"He's a good worker but isn't interested in social-political engagement with the union-"

I waved a hand at him, bored already. "OK, if I asked him a straight question, would I get a straight answer?"

"Depends," the union rep was thoughtful.

"Depends on what?"

"Whether he likes the look of you."

Mentally, I'd already discounted Westhäuser, and I headed back to the bus stop with the intention of going to see see the next name on the list: Heidemarie Müller, the goody two-shoes of the Party.

The next train was due in twenty minutes which gave me a bit of time pacing up and down the platform, thinking things through. I was testing out a theory in my head: what if the Boss only *thought* he and Sylvie Hofmann had been seen by Westhäuser when he was delivering drinks to the store in Wolzig? I was satisfied Westhäuser couldn't have been doing a delivery that day, yet the Boss had also convinced me that he hadn't got his dates mixed up. Perhaps Hofmann had made some chance remark about her neighbour working for VEB Likörfabrik Zernsdorf, maybe she'd even said it the day they went to Wolzig. She could have seen the lorry, mentioned it then. Who knew?

But if the Boss had seen the truck with the Liqueur factory stencil on the doors he might have made a point of checking the number plate. He would have come up with Westhäuser's name and decided to add it to my list.

If you ask me, with all my years of following, filming and interrogating people, the above explanation is not only the best one, but the only one that fits the known facts. It made for a nice little theory, but it raised a question that I hadn't got an answer for. Why would the Boss go to all that trouble? Tracking down a name on the off-chance that the person the name belonged to might have seen something? Bit too careful for my taste. Paranoid.

The railcar shunted up and I climbed aboard, moving my thoughts to Heidemarie Müller and the questions I would ask her.

12
NIEDERLEHME

I didn't expect any great problems with Heidemarie Müller, the model socialist citizen. Before leaving home this morning I'd phoned her workplace to check her shift patterns, so I knew she'd be there.

She worked at KIM—a factory farm. I'd been to a few of them in the course of my career and I'd learnt that there's no way to prepare yourself for those places. When I got to the gate I could hear machinery, tractors, fans humming. But the hundreds of thousands of broiler birds being reared and slaughtered here didn't seem to make any noise at all. I knew they were there because of the stink that thickened the closer I got to the plant. A smell like that grabs you by the neck, forces you to your knees and with one hand still on your throat it uses the other to twist your nose off by the roots. That's the kind of stink I'm talking about.

I flashed my disc and was directed to the switchboard room. I spotted Müller straight off thanks to the photo in her file. She was a demure little thing, mousy hair, big eyes lowered as I requested an audience.

We ended up in the break room, and I started with niceties: how the Party membership candidature was going, what her work entailed, how she got on with her colleagues.

Then I asked her about Sylvie Hofmann.

"Sylvie?" asked Müller. "Is this about Sylvie?"

I was so distracted by the delicate bouquet of chicken shit that I missed how Müller turned her face away at the mention of Hofmann.

What was Frau Hofmann's recent mental state? Did she talk about any difficulties at home?

Müller was conscientious in fulfilling her responsibility to assist the organs of the state but you couldn't accuse her of being a gossip. It took all my patience and years of interrogation experience to get the full story out of her.

Until recently, Müller and Hofmann hadn't been mere workmates, they'd spent a lot of time outside work together. Hofmann hadn't been getting along with hubby and had been glad of any time away from him.

"But something changed, a few months back I guess. We didn't meet up so much any more."

Müller blamed herself. The Party was demanding more of her time, she had to study the old dialectic materialism and learn her Lenin quotes, go to meetings and look both engaged and engaging. Couldn't blame her for thinking it was her fault, who'd want a square like that as best friend? But I didn't enlighten her that the real reason Hofmann started getting distracted two months ago was because she'd hooked up with my Boss.

"Have you met Hofmann at all outside work in the last couple of months?"

Müller gave me more guff about how diligent she was in her Party duties. I took that as a no.

"Did Hofmann ever talk to you about it? Maybe she gave reasons for spending less time with you?"

"No, I've already told you, it was me who had less free time. I feel guilty about that, but the Party is my priority."

"Do you two still talk? About life, relationships? Maybe during breaks here at work?"

She gave me a strange look, one that made me feel stupid. I swallowed and remained silent. Let her fill the gap. And after about thirty seconds, she did.

"I haven't seen Sylvie since Friday. She hasn't been to work," she explained. "The brigade leader doesn't know whether to be angry or worried."

I probed a bit: anyone checked whether she was at home, ill? Had there been any indication that she was about to take time off?

The brigadier had been round to Sylvie Hofmann's house, but no answer. The Hofmanns didn't have a phone, but Müller had phoned a neighbour a few times, but when the neighbour went round with a message there was never any answer.

Satisfied with Müller's answers and desperate to get away from the stink that hung over that place in the same way the smell of fear hovers over our interrogation rooms, I ticked her off my list and left.

As I walked down the hill to the bus stop, preoccupied with the question of why Hofmann had been playing truant, the air around me cleared a bit, but the whiff of rotting ammonia still clung to my clothes. I swore I'd never eat broiler chicken again.

The bus pulled in, the partially burnt hydrocarbons greasily swamping the smell of chicken shit, and I got on as a dame in a flowery nylon pinny got off. I was in my own head, working out my next steps and it was only when I sat down and wiped a peep-hole in the sooty window that I saw who had got off the bus: Dittmann, witness number one and assistant at the *Konsum* department store. This sure was a small town.

★

46

Twenty minutes later I was outside the Hofmann's single-storey grey-brick house. On the way here I'd checked the letter boxes nailed on a wooden frame at the end of the road—the Hofmann's box was stuffed so full that I was able to fish the top few letters out. Nothing exciting, just bills in Lutz Hofmann's name, pay slips for each of them. A postcard of Lake Balaton in Hungary—holiday greetings and best wishes from Gisela.

At the Hofmann's front gate I rang the bell, an old brass button fastened to the fence with a piece of electrical wire. From inside the house I heard a broken buzzing—the doorbell. I pressed the button again, the same cracked clapper, but no other sound.

I took a quick look around before vaulting over the fence. The front door got the benefit of a good banging, but there was still no answer, then I went round the house, looking through the windows. I could see used pans in the kitchenette, and a single plate and related cutlery on the table. Some apples lay in a bowl on the table, next to them the *Märkische Volksstimme* newspaper.

Another window showed me an unmade bed with an old-fashioned wooden frame and a suitcase lying open on top of it. A few clothes lying haphazardly around, as if taken from the open wardrobe. A bit further along and I found myself back at the front door. No side doors, no entrances to cellars. A garage stood to one side, the doors locked, windows opaque.

The next step was to go and see the gossipy neighbour I'd met the day before. That bit wasn't too hard—she was leaning out of her window watching me, nice and comfy with arms resting on a cushion. I jumped over the fence again and walked along the sandy strip by the side of the road until I got to her property.

"May I come in?" I called from the gate, ever so polite.

The babushka nodded, and I walked down the path until I was level with her viewing window.

"Afternoon." I did that stupid little salute the People's Police do, flat right hand, touch forefinger to right temple. Any further over and I'd be doing the Young Pioneer salute they make the kids do.

We introduced ourselves. My name for the day was *Obermeister der Kriminalpolizei* Teichert. The veteran's ID card told me she was called Zabel.

"Citizen Zabel, do you know when Sylvie Hofmann left?"

"Haven't seen her since Monday."

"And her husband, what day did you say you last saw him?"

The woman took another look at me. "Do we know each other?"

"Yesterday, ma'am. You were telling me how Frau Hofmann was upset about her husband." The brassy detective badge flashed in the low sunlight, but she didn't bother looking at it.

"Saw him Friday morning, on the way to work."

"And in the evening? Did you see him come home?"

She shook her head. She might be old and bent, but she seemed sharp enough.

"Last time we talked you said you hadn't seen Lutz Hofmann since Saturday."

"I did not!" She shook her head in disgust at the insinuation. "I told you that Frau Hofmann said her husband had been missing since Saturday."

An old trick, give them a slightly different version of what they've already told you and you can check how clear and truthful their memory is. The old biddy had passed with flying colours.

"Do the Hofmanns often go away?"

"Only on holiday. Sometimes they spend a few days with family." The babushka was packing away her cushion now, signalling that the audience was at an end.

"Family?" I didn't want to let her go just yet.

"In Berlin."

"Names, addresses?"

"Relatives of hers. Look them up on those lists you have."

13
REIM

Can you remember back to the beginning of this shaggy dog tale? The bit where I said that what got me up in the morning was the prospect of leaning on suspects? If you've been listening carefully, you'll have noticed that's true enough. But there's another couple of things about me that you should know. When the mood takes me I can be as contrary as a dissident who's been thrown out of the Gulag for bad behaviour. And the best way to get me in a contrary way is to make me do something stupid then refuse to explain precisely why it's not actually stupid. If you'd asked me yesterday whether I was wasting my time out there in the sticks I'd have told you how stupid I think the whole situation is. But things looked very different today.

Which brings me onto the second thing. Can't abide injustice. Go on then, laugh. Yeah, I work for the Firm, and sure, hereabouts the general impression of the Ministry for State Security is that we're a load of thugs and lowlifes on the make. In the non-socialist economies they have Mafia mobs; over here, they say, we have the Stasi.

I'm not going to argue the toss with you, I don't agree with that assessment, but what's the point of discussing it when you've already made your mind up? Sure, there are bad apples in the Ministry, same as there are bad apples in any organisation. But everything we do is in the interests of socialism. We protect the Workers' and Peasants' State. That simple.

But let's get back to me. Standing on the platform of KW station, waiting for an S-Bahn back to civilisation, I could smell injustice. It stank as high as that chicken factory I'd visited earlier in the day.

The whole thing was crooked from the get-go. The Boss sent me off to clean up his personal mess on the Firm's time—and let's not even get into the fact that the Boss's affair itself was jeopardising the good name of the Ministry. We'll sweep all that under the carpet—that kind of thing shouldn't happen, but it does. And let's face it, none of the *Bonzen* were ever going to get their knickers in a twist over something like that, not considering what they were all doing to their secretaries.

It's true, I was getting pissed off because whatever I did, I wasn't getting those loose ends tied. In fact, I was making them fray more and more. Both Hofmanns had gone missing, and then this whole thing about Berg? He was so frightened he couldn't talk. He struck me as being a doughty enough lad—had to be if he was going to deal with all the shit we tossed at exiteers like him. Something or someone had got to him, big time.

So what was so interesting about this particular job? It wasn't anything to do with my contrariness, nor was it about my overdeveloped sense of justice.

I smelled kompromat.

In my game there are basically three ways you can get someone to do what you want them to. You can appeal to their patriotism or any other conviction they might have. That's the best way, because it sticks.

The next option is the obvious one: violence and the threat of violence. In my book, it's overrated and over-

51

used because it's fun. But let's face it, it rarely works as well as people think it should.

Finally you've got good old blackmail. So far I'd never passed up the chance of looking for and using compromising material, and that policy had proved itself time and again. Right now there was good material hiding just below the surface of this case—I could tell because it was tickling my nose.

If I was prepared to take the risk and dig down far enough, I'd be sure to find gold; gold that one day might be useful against the Boss.

14

BERLIN FRIEDRICHSHAIN

When I got home my wife had made herself comfortable in my armchair. I looked at the flat-door and at the key and decided I needed to get better locks fitted.

"Renate? What the hell are you doing here?" I asked, still standing by the door.

"You smoked your birthday cigar?" She'd tidied away the empty bottle of Bulgarian wine and cleaned the ashtray.

"What are you doing here?" I had no problem repeating the question because I really wanted to know the answer.

"Saxony sucks," she answered, as if that were enough reason to come marching back into my life after a year of separation.

"So does Berlin, but I notice that hasn't stopped you dropping by."

"Oh, Hans-Peter, always were the joker, weren't you."

Nobody calls me Hans-Peter. Even my own mother calls me Reim. And I wasn't a joker, either. I was deadly serious. I crossed the room in two strides and grabbed Renate by the arm. I jerked her out of the armchair and dragged her towards the door.

"Where's your stuff? Did you bring a suitcase?" I shoved her, hard enough that her face hit the wall with a satisfying thud, and while she was still thinking about that I went into the bedroom where I found her suitcase on the bed.

I picked it up, but before I'd got as far as the hallway she was standing in front of me.

"Fröhlich sent me," she said, getting it out before I laid into her again.

That brought me up short. "The Boss?"

"Not him in person, he sent one of his lackeys with the message." She took the suitcase out of my stiff hand and took it back into the bedroom. "Said the Ministry liked to see its officers happily married. I told him I couldn't make that happen, and he suggested that living under the same roof would be enough." She'd opened the case up and was taking clothes out, laying them across the bed.

"What's in it for you?"

"Fröhlich said if I came back to you then you'd get a promotion."

"Very nice. What's in it for you?"

She looked up from sorting clothes and gave me a pitying smile. "If I move back in I can do my shopping in the store at the Ministry, and if you get promoted then I get access to a wider range of consumer goods, and more money to spend, too."

"That's it? You're prepared to move back in just so you can go shopping?"

"If you'd been to Löbau these last ten years then you'd know what the shops down there are like. Queue for an hour and when you get inside the shelves are practically empty." She opened a drawer, took my socks out, and dumped them on the floor to make room for her own underclothes.

"Any other reason?"

"Oh yes, my mother's been driving me up the wall," she said lightly.

I left her unpacking and went for a shower. While I

waited for the water to run warm, I took off and threw my crumpled suit, still stinking of bird shit, in the corner. It would need a damn good wash before I wore it again. When I got out, the bedroom door was closed and a pillow and blanket were waiting for me on the sofa.

15

BERLIN ALEXANDERPLATZ

The wife woke me the next morning, clearing away the full ashtray, the empty glass and the bottle with a couple of fingers of *Kornschnaps* still in it.

"Stop that damn noise!"

Renate stood there, tapping her wristwatch. Only when she was satisfied that I'd got her not-so-subtle hint did she move into the kitchen to bang around a bit more.

Once again, I went to see the Boss first thing, waiting outside his office at seven on the dot. He let me in, and while I spoke, he added notes in the margins of a file. I didn't mention the reappearance of my wife, I concentrated on making my report on the operation in Königs Wusterhausen. The Boss, however had different ideas. He shut the file he'd been reading and looked up at me.

"Are those four witnesses prepared to swear they've never seen me and Citizen Hofmann within a hundred metres of each other?"

It was one of his rhetorical questions and I didn't answer. I also didn't press the point I was trying to make about things being a little more complicated than he was prepared to admit.

You might say I'm a coward. Me? I'd tell you my behaviour is consistent with the concept of personal development in accordance with the teachings of dialectic materialism. Lenin would have applauded my approach—when your opponent has the upper hand, work underground.

The Boss was in a mood to quote Lenin too: "There are decades when nothing happens; and there are weeks when decades happen," he told me, dismissing my report. He wanted me to follow up the names that were still on the list, but in a rare concession, he said he was prepared to wait a little longer.

"You want me to bring Berg and Westhäuser in?" I decided to check.

"Wait a day or two, give Berg one more chance. If he doesn't cough up, bring him in. I want to know what he knows so I can decide what to do with him"

"And the lorry driver."

"Oh, forget about him." It looked like the Boss had accepted that Westhäuser hadn't been in Wolzig that day. "Don't you have work to do?" he asked.

I stood up, saluted and left his presence.

I certainly did have work to do, but not in the way the Boss meant. I went back to my desk, made a couple of quick phone calls, poured myself a small glass of hair of the dog and took out the packet of cigarettes. Once the *Nordhäuser Doppelkorn* had slid down and the f6 was sparked up I felt a bit more in control. I scanned through the notes I'd made the other day when Holger got me those files, looking for Sylvie Hofmann's maiden name. There she was: Wilde. After I'd found that out I treated myself to another bit of hair of dog, just to keep myself sharp.

★

Flap my clapper in the direction of the sentry at the main gate, holding my breath in case he smelt the fusel, and down the road to the S-Bahn station.

When the ivory and burgundy train ground in, I boarded and found myself a seat. The person opposite got up at the next stop. I watched out of the corner of my eye as he checked whether I was looking before discreetly finding himself another place to sit.

I got out and dived into the bustle of life that is Alexanderplatz. Turning my back on the tourists admiring the World Clock and the Telespargel, I crossed the road on the way to the *Präsidium*, the Berlin police HQ.

I didn't have to wait long before Georg, an old mate, came out to meet me. We did our national service together, and stayed in touch because it suited both of us to share operationally significant information from time to time. He tipped me off whenever a sensitive case landed on his desk, which meant gold stars for me when I passed that information along. In return I give him the heads up when I heard about any upcoming checks on the political reliability of officers in his department.

There were other benefits to the relationship, like right now I wanted to check the register of residents, but couldn't do that back at the big house in Lichtenberg. The Boss would find out about it inside of ten minutes. I passed the two names along to Georg and sent him off to population records.

I killed time by counting the floors of the *Interhotel Stadt Berlin*. I knew exactly how many there were: 36, plus another three at the bottom with a much larger footprint. If you're interested I could tell you how many rooms (1006) and how many beds (1982) there were, along with how many are permanently wired for sound (126, but microphones can be set up within half an hour in all other rooms). After all, it's my job to know these things, along with the statistics for all the other hotels where Westerners and delegates from the fraternal socialist states stay when visiting the Capital of the GDR.

Georg came back with the information I needed. I put the pieces of paper he gave me in my briefcase and we shook hands.

16
KÖNIGS WUSTERHAUSEN

I bought an extra deck of cigarettes at the station, and after a moment's hesitation, added a box of matches to my purchases—they only cost ten Pfennigs. There wasn't anything I had to say to Berg, I just wanted him to know that I hadn't forgotten him. A purely friendly visit, hence the ciggies.

I found Berg tinkering with the rollers on a belt conveyor. He looked up as he heard me approaching and stood up, arms loose by his side, a 32 millimetre ring spanner in one hand. I knew it was a 32 millimetre ring spanner because he held it up in front of my mug and told me.

"There's a shortage of these," he waved the spanner at me. Not in an aggressive way, but I kept my distance anyway. "What kind of country can't even cover its own need for spanners?"

He opened his other hand, showing me a slim strip of metal.

"I have to use this as a shim because the bolts are all different sizes. Is it any wonder that so many of us have had enough of this place?"

I took the nails from my pocket, pulled one out with my lips and held the pack out to Berg. He put the spanner and shim on the belt and took his time choosing which cigarette he was going to take. When he'd finally settled on one he leaned in to catch a spark from the lit match I was cupping in my hand.

"What have I done to deserve a visit?" he asked after inhaling and holding the smoke for a second or two.

"Hope I'm not keeping you from work?"

"Ha!" Berg pointed his cigarette at the spanner and shim. "Actually it's nice to have an excuse not to work, not like they can sack me or anything."

"Not unless we ask them to," I suggested.

Berg didn't have an answer to that. He didn't care any more. We'd taken his profession from him and made him work in one of the shittiest jobs in the area—mind you, it could have been worse: I've heard some of the jobs in the open-cast lignite mines are no fun. Or any of the factories in Leuna, Bitterfeld or Buna. But Berg was biding his time until we decided to let him leave.

"Have you thought about what we talked about the other day?" I asked.

"We talked about lots of things. Got another *Kippe* for me?"

I took out another cigarette, but held it just out of his reach. He hadn't finished the first one, anyway. "What happened Friday night? What did you see."

"I didn't see anything." He held his hand out for the cigarette. "Not unless you're bigger than whatever it is I didn't see."

"Just so happens I might be." I flipped open my Ministry pass. "Will that do you?"

"Rank?" He asked.

Believe it or not, the rank of a Stasi officer is classified, which is why neither my name nor my rank was on the same page as my mugshot. That page proved I was the legitimate holder of a currently valid pass, no more and no less. But right now I was in the business of building trust with Berg.

"Major," I lied.

"Major? A major wouldn't be out here doing this kind of legwork. I'd have you pegged as a *Feldwebel*."

A sergeant. Ouch.

"Let's just say we're taking a special interest in what happened last Friday."

"What do I get?"

"I've already told you. We expedite your exit process, and in the meantime the local lads will go easy on you. Not too easy, mind, we don't want people talking."

He took the cigarette from me and chained it off the embers of the last one. He turned away to do it, and used the time to do some thinking about my offer. After half a cigarette, which wasn't a very long time considering how he smoked, he turned back.

"OK, I don't believe you're an officer. Prove to me you're not just an *Uffzi*." He still thought I was an NCO.

He expected me to show him a different page of my pass, the one with my name and rank. But I did better than that, I told him the very last thing he expected me to know.

"Last Friday you saw our Soviet brothers in action."

Berg dropped his cigarette and looked around, checking nobody was near. I'd done it, I'd convinced him.

I couldn't let it show, but mentally I was congratulating myself at the guess. It wasn't really a guess, I'd had time to think about it, and the only thing that might frighten an intelligent young man like Berg more than my Firm were our Russian Friends. Now I just had to tickle the details out of him.

"You can't protect me."

"I'm a major. And now you know I am, because an NCO or lower ranking officer wouldn't have the information I've just disclosed."

"Cigarette," he demanded.

I gave him the whole pack, felt easier than doling them out one by one. I also gave him time to think a bit more. Best not to rush this next bit.

"OK. What do you want to talk to me about?"

"Tell me, in your own words, what you saw last Friday. We need to confirm a few facts before we confront the Friends."

"You won't get anywhere with them!"

"Let me worry about that. But I'll tell you this, what you saw on Friday wasn't sanctioned by the Soviet Army. Which is why they asked us to help with investigations. You're safe. We won't tell them about you."

Berg leaned back against the conveyor and breathed out so heavily that he started coughing. He ground out his cigarette on the belt behind him and lit another.

"I didn't see much. I was driving home after my shift-"

"What time was that?"

"Be about quarter past, twenty past eleven? You know that road through the Tiergarten? It's narrow, the woods come right up to the edge. I saw a UAZ jeep pulled up on the side of the road. It was canted at an angle, on the left side of the road. There's a gully. I slowed down, curiosity mainly, I don't think I would have stopped even if they'd needed help—you hear these stories about the Russians. As it was, I saw movement in the light of my headlights. Men moving around, so I knew they were OK."

He took another cigarette out of the packet and twisted it between thumb and forefinger.

"I don't normally smoke this much, it's just ... Well, I was almost past them. A car came the other way, and the headlights from that car lit up the scene like it was a play. I could see everything."

"What did you see?"

"Two men. Carrying a body into the woods."

"Describe them."

"One had his back to me. Not nearly as tall as the other, or as wide. Short and wiry, I'd say. He had a greatcoat on."

"And the other?"

"Big. Bigger than you, with a square head. Bald he was, with a moustache."

"You saw all that?" I checked.

Berg tapped his temple. "All in here. Branded into memory. Can't get rid of it."

I knew someone who fitted the description Berg had given me. Someone who had already told me he was in the area on Friday evening.

I fetched the photograph of the Boss out of my briefcase.

"This your man?" I asked.

Berg dropped his cigarette and took a step back, colliding with the conveyor belt. "That's him."

17
ZERNSDORF

With the new information from Berg, my attention returned to Hofmann. The theory I was going with for the moment was that the Boss and Sylvie Hofmann were the ones carrying the body—presumably that of Hofmann's husband—into the woods that Friday night.

I returned to Zernsdorf and, safe in the knowledge that Westhäuser was at work, I let myself into his apartment. Picking his lock took no more than a minute or two, and during that time I was unbothered by neighbours. Once in his flat I took a quick look around. It didn't take long, just the one room with kitchen niche, plus lobby-hall and a small bathroom. Furniture seemed to be hard to come by in Westhäuser's world—he made do with a table, an easy chair and a bed. He more than made up for the scarce furnishings with the drinks crates standing in all corners. I lifted a bottle out: Vita Cola. He didn't even have the decency to get beer in for any thirsty visitors that might drop by.

What his flat did offer was a perfect view of the Hofmanns' house, along with those of their neighbours. Zabel, the old biddy next-door-but-one was clearing up leaves, shovelling them into a pile in the corner. It took her a long time to drag her broken body after the rake, and I began to think that I'd be spending the rest of the day watching the veteran clear up her garden.

I took the opportunity to look at the list of addresses that my friend Georg had procured for me. Have you any idea how many Hofmanns and Hoffmanns there are in Berlin? Six pages of small print. I'd had no major expectations from the exercise, but knew that the list might come in useful if and when I narrowed the field a little.

My reading was interrupted by the whir of a Wartburg engine. I looked up in time to see the car pull up in front of Zabel's house, and she opened the gate for the driver, a young woman. The two of them disappeared into the house, emerging a quarter of an hour later. Zabel no longer had her pinny on, she was dressed in going-out clothes, and held a shopping basket in the crook of her arm. Zabel and the woman drove off. Before the exhaust fumes had cleared I was down the stairs and across the road to the Hofmanns'.

I vaulted the garden gate and put my picks to work on the front door lock. This one was even easier than Westhäuser's and I clicked it open in record time.

Normally on a search like this there would be a team of investigators. The status quo would first be documented with notes and pictures from instant cameras, then, wearing gloves, the team would take the place apart before putting it back together again exactly as it had been before.

Little old me had no team and no camera, just myself and my cotton gloves. I first went through the house, getting a general impression, and took a few moments in the bedroom, comparing it with the pictures I held in my memory. Cupboard, chest of drawers with knick-knacks on top and the old-fashioned wooden bed. The suitcase and strew of clothes were still on the bed, the cupboard doors were still open. Everything was as it had been the previous day when I had peered in through the windows. I was quite certain no-one had been here in the meantime.

My next destination was the writing desk under the window in the living room. It was an antique bureau, the roll-top pushed back to expose the writing surface and pigeon holes. I gently lifted a sheaf of bills, looking underneath for a writing case or pad of writing paper, but found none. Turning my attention to the small compartments, I used a finger to lift each sheet of paper, peering in to gain an impression of what it was. More bills, union membership book, correspondence with the town council. I was about to turn my attention to the trays in the pillar cupboards either side of the knee-hole when I heard a ratcheting click from outside.

Straightening up just enough to peer over the windowsill, I saw Sylvie Hofmann walking down the garden path. I slipped into the bedroom and took cover under the bed.

The door snipped open and Sylvie came into the house. She went straight to the living room, and I could hear a light door being opened, perhaps one in the writing desk? A rustle of papers, then footsteps heading in my direction. The bed sagged as she sat on it, springs scratching my cheek as they shifted under her weight. I could see her shoes, planted firmly on the floor just a few centimetres from my shoulder.

There was silence for a good while, maybe fifteen or twenty seconds, then she sighed and the springs lifted away from my face and the shoes moved over to the chest of drawers. Clothes pulled out and thrown on the bed as Hofmann shifted between drawers and cupboard several times, each time adding more to the pile. Finally she stood next to the bed, sorting her belongings, the bed creaking and bellying down on to me every time she pressed more items into the case.

She lifted the suitcase and stood by the door for a few moments, feet pointed towards me, then with another sigh she left the room.

Thirty seconds later the front door closed, followed shortly by the snicker of the garden gate.

18
ZERNSDORF

I slid out from under the bed and looked out of the living room window. I could just see Hofmann disappearing towards the railway station. I checked my watch, fifteen minutes until the train to KW was due.

Not for the first time, I cursed the Boss for not letting me bring a car, and ran through my options. Because of the first rule of covert surveillance—that anonymity is the greatest asset and therefore cover should never be voluntarily blown—tailing Hofmann on foot was a non-starter, the house stood just before a bend in the road, and after that it was dead straight almost all the way to the station—there was no way to trail her and not be blown, at least not without keeping a fair amount of distance between us.

Assuming she really was heading for the station, I wouldn't need to trail her, I could follow her at my leisure and pick up her trail on the train. That gave me just less than five minutes to complete my search of the house and leave.

I rifled the desk, looking for addresses or correspondence with friends or family in Berlin. I worked quickly, no longer worried about leaving a mess, but still came up with nothing. Not even a diary or address book. I went into the kitchen to check the drawers there, then a last, desperate search of the drawers in the bedroom which turned up nothing but handkerchiefs and clothes.

I let myself out, and satisfied nobody was to be seen on the street, I climbed the garden gate and jogged away.

The station master was just opening the gate as I arrived, and passengers were walking over to the platform. A V100 diesel was wheezing its way towards us, pulling three carriages and leaving a trail of black smoke behind. When it arrived, I got into a different carriage from Hofmann, but stood near the connecting door where I could keep an eye on her through the window.

Satisfied that Hofmann was settled in her seat, I retreated a few steps, only moving closer to the connecting door when we arrived at Niederlehme station. Hofmann stayed put, and as the train pulled out I went to stand closer to the exit, keen to be the first off the train when we arrived at Königs Wusterhausen.

The S-Bahn was waiting on the other side of the platform, and Hofmann crossed between the trains without even glancing around. I let her find a seat before I climbed aboard and sat myself down at the far end of the same carriage. I was unable to see her because of the compartment dividers adjacent to each set of doors, but she'd placed her suitcase in the aisle, and I kept my eyes on that.

If the journey from KW into Berlin was normally boring, this trip was skull-crushingly monotonous. I couldn't allow myself to look out of the window or invent backstories for my fellow passengers, and every time we neared a station my attention would sharpen and my muscles coil, ready for sudden movement. But Hofmann didn't play any tricks. Her suitcase remained in the aisle until we pulled out of Jannowitzbrücke when she stood up, picked up her suitcase and, with natural casualness, went to stand by the doors.

The next station, Alexanderplatz, teems with travellers at any time of the day; I'd have to keep my wits about me if I wanted to remain on her trail. Alone as I was, I'd need to stay close, no more than two or three people behind her. Any further back and Hofmann could easily disappear into the crowds before I had a chance to get around any ditherers blocking my path.

Hofmann paused at the top of the stairs to the station concourse below, putting her suitcase down and flexing her hand. She picked the suitcase up again and made her way down the steps, turning left at the bottom and heading straight for the nearest exit.

Once we were out of the station the crowds evaporated, and I had to allow some distance to develop. I stopped to light a cigarette, watching as she crossed in front of the taxi stand and disappeared into the Centrum department store. Dropping my freshly-lit cigarette, I ran across the road, and followed Hofmann into the store, stopping at the door to get my bearings. A moment of panic while I scanned the shoppers and assistants, searching for Hofmann and her suitcase. No show. A second scan, this time while I was moving towards the central staircase that led up to the other floors. I climbed a few steps to gain some height, checking the heads of the shoppers below me, my eyes lingering on every blonde woman that was about Hofmann's age—it was a good vantage point, but I could see less than half the shop floor from here, and she wasn't in my field of vision. Should I go back down to check the rest of the ground floor, or upstairs to the other levels?

I turned and ran up the stairs to the first floor, and slowing my pace only a little, I made a circuit of the glass and ceramics department before moving into household goods. Up another level, ladies' wear. I took this floor more slowly, checking beneath the curtains of the changing booths. There, the one in the corner, that was Hofmann's suitcase pressed against the curtain—I strode over and yanked the curtain open.

"How dare you, young man!" a grey-haired veteran slapped me about the shoulders and face with a clothes hanger, then pulled back the curtain and began to scream for help.

I left the department store, pronto. Let's face it, I'd lost Hofmann.

19
BERLIN TREPTOW

It was shift change, and as the S-Bahn rattled its way towards Schöneweide the carriage filled up. Railway workers slick with diesel and grimy with coal; dock workers from the Osthafen, dusty from the grain hoppers; metal workers from the fridge factory. I ignored them all, knowing my corner of the carriage was safe from intruders.

But someone slumped into the seat opposite me. I had a look at his mush. He was nearing retirement. His hair was lank from sweat, metal filings and dried oil clogged the creases in his heavy face and hung onto bushy eyebrows above deep, grey eyes.

He reminded me of my old tutor, Major Renn. Back in the day, when I was a candidate officer doing my schooling at the MfS high school in Golm, Renn had come into classes, caterpillar eyebrows alive. He taught me practically the only useful thing I learned in that place (other than how to fix people): when you're stuck, go back to the beginning.

Back at the Clubhouse I sat at my desk, surrounded by pillars of folders that I should have been working on. Instead, my focus was on the sparse notes I'd made when reading the files on the Boss's witnesses.

Major Renn was right: after carefully re-reading my

notes I came up with several suggestions for myself. Chief among them: pay more attention.

Dittmann's son-in-law was called Müller, as was Hofmann's colleague, Heidemarie. It's only the most common name in our Republic so you may forgive me for not noticing the coincidence straight off. But I wasn't in such a forgiving mood.

I'd been in a rush, keen to capture the salient facts so hadn't copied out more than the barest details. Now I regretted my haste. I'd have to take another trip to KW to check whether or not the shared name really was a simple coincidence.

The second thing I thought about when reading the notes was that Heidemarie Müller might be better informed than neighbour Zabel when it came to knowing who Hofmann's friends and relations in Berlin might be.

I checked my watch, I could be back in KW by 1700. Müller would have clocked off work by then and I could interview her at home. Meaning I wouldn't have to go to the chicken factory.

20
NIEDERLEHME

Heidemarie Müller lived in a housing block sandwiched between the KIM broilers and the Berliner Ring motorway.

"If the wind comes from the west or the north the noise from the motorway keeps us awake. If it's from the south or the east we get the smell from KIM," she told me as she let me into the narrow hallway.

"What happens if there's no wind," I asked, trying for friendly interest.

"Then we get both."

The first surprise was waiting for me in the living room. Frau Dittmann was sitting there, presiding over a table set for coffee and cake.

"Frau Dittmann," I shook hands. It seemed I was always playing nice cop these days. I'd have to be careful the wind didn't change, and not just because of the stink from the chickens.

"*Mutti*, would you pick the children up?" Heidemarie ignored the disappointment on her mother's coupon and shut the door after her.

I was making good progress, I had one question answered even before the coffee had been poured.

"Coffee, Comrade *Obermeister?*" She was already pouring the coffee, but was sharp enough to notice my eyes sliding over to the drinks cabinet. "Shall I add a little something? *Goldbrand* do you?"

I looked at Müller with fresh eyes, willing to revise my first impressions of this modest and prim Party candidate.

"You live alone?" I held my cup out for a glug of the brandy-derived schnapps, and was gratified when Heidemarie added some to her own coffee, too.

"My mother is picking the children up from the Kindergarten. I threw my husband out when he applied for permission to leave the GDR."

"That shows great social responsibility."

"We wanted different things." Heidemarie shrugged.

"If you don't mind me asking, has his hostile attitude towards our state led to any problems with your Party candidature?"

"Of course. But I've started divorce proceedings and I'm hopeful I will be given a chance to show my loyalty."

Enough small talk, particularly this kind of small talk which, as I may have mentioned, gives me indigestion.

"I have a few questions about Frau Hofmann. Obviously we're keen to make sure nothing untoward has happened to her."

Heidemarie reached behind her and picked up a glass ashtray from the wall unit, a heavy round thing with a Martini logo in the centre. She was probably proud of this artefact from the West and only brought it out for special visitors. I gratefully lit up, and, after a puff I remembered my manners and pointed the deck in her direction. Her hand hovered for a moment, then fell back onto her lap.

"I've given up," she said. But I noticed her eyes following the glowing tip of my cigarette every time I raised it to my lips.

I could get to like a girl like Heidemarie.

I went through the motions, asking question upon question, the answers to which didn't interest me in the slightest. It served to bolster my cover as a detective from K, and to get her used to answering without thinking too much. Where did you do your vocational training? How long have you been working at KIM?

After a few warm-up questions I moved onto themes I was more interested in: when did you first get to know Sylvie Hofmann? What do you know about her relationship with her husband? What is your opinion of her husband?

These questions added background to my investigation, but right now I was most interested in where Hofmann might be holed up.

"Did you ever go to the capital with Citizen Hofmann?"

"She was good with the kids, she went with us to the *Kulturpark* and the museums."

"What about just the two of you? Girls' nights out, that kind of thing?"

Heidemarie poured herself another coffee, then, still leaning over the table, asked politely for a cigarette. I let her choose one and struck a match for her.

"Those were the days." She plucked a wisp of smoke from the cigarette, then held it vertically, the tip just a few centimetres in front of her eyes. The smoke curled up between us.

I gave her and the cigarette a moment to get acquainted while I poured myself another coffee.

"Tell me about the days."

"One of those underground clubs up in Prenzlauer Berg, or we'd dress up and pretend we might get into Cafe Moskau." She laughed into the smoke and gave the butt another nip.

"And did you always manage to catch the last S-Bahn home?"

"Last train?" Her pupils dilated as she shifted her focus

through the smoke to look at me. "Sylvie and I could dance until morning!"

"So you didn't ever stay over in Berlin?"

"Are you trying to insinuate something? Because if you are, you're not doing it very well."

"I'm sorry. What I meant was, did you ever stay at friends or relatives of Sylvie's?" I'd been clumsy in my questioning, so now I had to work harder to placate her.

Heidemarie thought about it a little, her attention back on the helix of smoke spiralling upwards through shafts of sunlight. "There was somewhere, maybe in Schöneweide?"

"An address, perhaps?" Heidemarie shook her head, and I tried to narrow things down, "Near the station, or over the river?"

"Near the station. New build it was. Down the steps, the ones that come out under the bridge, turn right, and somewhere round there. An aunt, perhaps? I didn't actually see her, we arrived late and by the time we got up the next morning the aunt had gone to work."

"Do you ever visit Sylvie at home?"

"She came round here more often, it was a way for her to put off the inevitable."

I sipped my coffee, waiting for her to give me more information.

"Things aren't so good with Lutz, her husband," she whispered, as if Hofmann might be next door, listening to our conversation.

"Is he violent?" I asked, taking care over my tenses.

"She never talks about it, but yes, she's had a few black eyes and sore fingers over the years."

"Did she ever report this?"

Heidemarie moved the hand holding her cigarette to one side and crossed one leg over the other. She'd kicked off her house shoes and I could see her toes beneath the webbing of her tights.

"I never asked."

I didn't have much time left, Dittmann and the kids had returned, I could hear the kerfuffle from the lobby.

"When you went to Berlin, did you ever stay anywhere else?"

"Yeah, we stayed near Ostkreuz a few times. She said it was some kind of cousin but she shared his bedroom and I got the couch. And no, I don't remember the address."

"Would you be able to find the place again?"

"Maybe ... Yeah, think so." Heidemarie leant over to stub out her cigarette, giving me a view down her décolletage. "Would you like me to take you?"

21
BERLIN FRIEDRICHSHAIN

The warm glow of a Narva light bulb welcomed me home. For a moment I wondered whether I'd left it on by mistake when I went to work this morning, then I remembered my wife.

"Renate, is dinner ready?" I could see the table in the corner was empty but I asked anyway. If I had to have her under my roof she could at least make herself useful.

"I've eaten, thanks," she called from my bedroom.

The blanket, sheet and pillow that I'd used last night had been folded and carefully piled up at the end of the sofa. The rest of the place looked pretty tidy, too. I didn't care much about orderliness but I did care about the hole in my belly.

"I've been at work all day, will you come and make me my dinner?"

The creak of bed springs, then Renate appeared in the bedroom doorway. She gave me a cool look then took herself off to the kitchen and started cutting bread, sausage and some veg.

I switched the television on, sat myself on the couch, put my feet on the table, lit up and waited for *Aktuelle Kamera* and the lovely newsreader, Angelika, with her impossibly glossy hair.

Renate made no attempt to be quiet about laying the table, even though she could see I was watching the news.

The beer bottle and the glass climpered as she plonked them on the table. The knives and the bread board clattered and if she could have made the slices of bread rattle then she would have done so.

"It's ready," she told me, standing in front of the telly.

"I'm watching this."

"Five minutes ago you were too starving to get your own tea, now all of a sudden you're so interested in what the Central Committee is saying about the five year plan that you don't want my food?"

She was right. I wasn't interested in the five year plan, and the beer was waiting for me.

"Will you eat with me?" I asked her.

She watched me pour the beer, then went to get her own bottle and a glass.

"You haven't changed," she said as she sat down.

"Neither have you."

I don't know why, but we both thought that was funny.

"How are you?" she asked after our grins had slipped.

"Work. Got a bad case on at the moment."

She knew better than to ask for details, and the conversation petered out. Angelika carried on reading the news in the corner. Another ten minutes and we could switch over to the bulletin on Western TV.

"Really that bad in Löbau?" I asked, wondering whether affability might suit me.

"Must be if moving back in with you is preferable."

"Your mum?"

"The whole thing. I missed Berlin. The town, the bustle. The people."

"You missed me, didn't you?"

"That's what you say."

I spread some *Leberwurst* on my bread, added some chopped onion. Drank some beer.

"I don't regret moving out," she said. "Just so you don't get the wrong idea."

I hadn't the slightest intention of getting the wrong idea. Renate had moved out nearly a year ago, as far as I was concerned it was completely unprovoked. I wasn't in the business of forgiving something like that.

"Hadn't thought about it," I told her.

"That's it, right there—you're just not interested! The very reason I left you."

"I'm sorry. Like I said, hard day. Hard week, actually. Peace offering?" I held out my half-eaten sandwich.

"It's always a hard day with you. How are we going to make a go of it if you're only interested in work and drinking?"

"Who said anything about making a go of it?"

"Your Boss did," she shot back.

"Well, in that case."

Once Renate had retreated behind the bedroom door to sulk, I moved to the couch with a piece of paper and a pencil. I'd told her the truth at dinner when I said I was having a hard time at work—it's not every day you find out your boss was involved in the disposal of a body, probably that of the husband of his girlfriend, the one who's given you the slip when you tried to follow her. I'd not had a chance to consider what I'd found out, I'd been on auto pilot ever since speaking to Berg. It's one thing to follow whatever leads I had without arousing the Boss's suspicion, it's another to find time to consider my next moves.

I wanted to have further confirmation that it really was the Boss that Berg had seen. He'd recognised the photo, and Fröhlich had already told me he was with Sylvie in the Tiergarten that night, so under normal circumstances that would have been more than enough. But like

82

everything else the last few days, these weren't normal circumstances—it was the Boss we were talking about.

I'd also need to check it was actually a body that he and the other person were carrying, and not a sack of garden waste.

I considered again whether the second person Berg had seen was actually Sylvie Hofmann. Berg's description matched her in terms of size and height: she was taller than average for a woman.

I rested my cigarette on the edge of the ashtray and made some notes:

Sylvie Hofmann with Fröhlich?
Body = Lutz Hofmann?

Who else could it be? The Boss was seeing Lutz Hofmann's wife, Heidemarie had told me Hofmann used to beat his wife. Plenty of potential for conflict right there. As a bonus clue: Lutz Hofmann went missing on Friday, latest Saturday morning.

Check with DVP for missing persons

I wasn't sure how to ask the local cops about missing persons, not without word getting back to Berlin. Perhaps Georg could help?

Ask Georg – check misper register

My cigarette had gone out, so I put the pencil down and sparked it up again, inhaling the tar-heavy fumes to help me think.

I needed to talk to Heidemarie again—the interview had been rushed and I'd jumped from theme to theme, trying to get the basic details out of her.

Make Heidemarie sweat some more

I was looking forward to another chat with that lady. And anyway, hadn't she given me the come-on right at the end, when she offered to show me where she and Silvie Hofmann had sometimes stayed?

I underlined the last point on my list.

22
POTSDAM

For the second morning running, I was woken by my inconsiderate wife—she has a medal for boiling water in the loudest possible way.

"You better get up if you want breakfast," she said from the kitchen. "I have to get to work."

"Work?" I rubbed my eyes and tried to focus on her.

"You can't expect me to sit around all day, waiting for my man to get home."

Turns out she was more pally with the Boss than I'd guessed—he'd found her a position in Medical Services at the Centre. While I was digesting that I sat up and looked for my socks. They'd gone. Along with all my other clothes. I looked a bit further and discovered a pile of fresh laundry on the table.

It wasn't until I'd struggled my way into the clean clothes that I remembered the notes I'd made last night. The ones that I, against all service regulations, had left lying around in the open. A quick look at the coffee table by the couch: there was the piece of paper, next to the beer bottles and the overflowing ashtray.

I checked Renate's attention was elsewhere and quickly folded the page and put it in my trouser pocket, pushing a handkerchief down on top of it.

"I'll have a coffee," I announced, then headed into the bathroom to wash my face.

Renate wanted to know if I was coming into the Centre today, but I fobbed her off and she left before me. Once she was safely out the door, I lifted the phone and made a short call to a number in Potsdam.

I hung up and caught the S-Bahn to Karlshorst where the 0712 *Sputnik* to Potsdam was waiting. I'd missed the commuter rush and the double-decker train carriage was as empty as a butcher's shelf in Löbau. The crumpled wrapper of a Rotstern bar of chocolate lay by my feet and I eyed it hungrily, wishing I'd had more than just coffee for breakfast. Instead of food I had my cigarettes with me, and during the journey I added a small pile of butts to the other rubbish on the scuffed floor.

Potsdam Hauptbahnhof was my destination, at least on this train. The station is actually just a busy railway junction several kilometres from the town, and I dithered on the lower platform for a moment: the shuttle train was the quickest way to the centre of Potsdam, but the tram passed nearer Park Sanssouci, where I had an appointment.

Potsdam is one of the places that Western tourists flock to, keen to see the refined pomposity of the Prussian past. Since my department's responsibilities are passport control and tourism—keeping an eye on any and all foreigners that cross our borders—Potsdam is a particularly interesting place for us. I may not have any informants in Königs Wusterhausen, but I have lots of connections in Potsdam. I'd found it difficult to make progress over the last few days but I'd do better here in the administrative centre of the district which covered KW and all those other sandpits I'd been forced to spend time in over the last few days.

It was still too early for the tourists, and I wandered

through the faded elegance of the park Lenné had laid out around the Charlottenhof palace. The air was cool under the trees, and the dew glimmered like the frost that would soon be here. The leaves on the trees were drying and turning, giving a papery rustle in the breeze as I walked towards the Hippodrom.

Captain Lang of the *Volkspolizei* was waiting for me in the centre of the landscaped clearing.

"There was a statue of Old Fritz right here," he said as I came up behind him. He was wearing his green policeman's uniform, looking at the spot where Frederick the Great had once stood. "Apparently it was rescued from Berlin just before it got smelted down. They brought it here and now you boys in Berlin have got him again. Welcome to him, far as I'm concerned."

"I need some help," I told him as we shook hands.

He gave me a measured look. "Not like you, Reim. Normally you come down here to pump us dry and give us more orders."

"I'm working on your territory right now, I need your connections."

The two of us set off at a slow pace, following the path around the edge of the Hippodrom. Lang was nervous, not in an obvious way, but I could tell by how he watched me out of the corner of his eye. He had good reason to be nervous: a couple of years ago some schoolkids in Potsdam were involved in organising a protest. I don't even remember what it was about, no doubt some revisionist nonsense that they'd heard about on Western TV. It wasn't anything to do with me, I'd just stumbled upon it while engaged in operational observation of a Westerner. Instead of passing it straight on to Department XX, I did a bit of digging. The kids were in the same class as Lang's daughter, and seeing my chance I took it with both hands. I told Lang that I had evidence his daughter was involved, explained in painful detail how she was destined for Hoheneck jail and how he was facing the end of his career in the *Volkspolizei*. I offered to keep the girl out of it. Providing, of course, that he remembered my good deed.

"There's a case in Königs Wusterhausen." I opened proceedings. "I need your operational co-operation. Inside gen, have a few people followed. The usual."

"Ask the lads in Department VIII—that's what they're there for."

"Not sure this one's got legs—want to check it out before I make it official."

We walked a round or two in silence while Lang thought things through. I could tell he wasn't happy about the request, but we'd worked together for years, and favours were a kind of currency in our business.

"Tell me what you need."

I gave him the list of names and my requirements.

"That it?" he asked when he'd finished noting it all down.

"I'd like a look at your missing persons registry, entries in the last month."

"Central Co-ordination at your ministry will already have a copy." Lang paused, then nodded in understanding. "You want to check this out before you make it official? OK, but you'll have to come down to the police station."

"I only need the entries for Königs Wusterhausen county—will you copy them out and bring them to me?"

"OK, meet me when I finish my shift. Let's say 1500."

★

Keen to have an official justification for my trip to Potsdam, I popped into the district's Department VI. Just like the Main Department in Berlin, Line VI here in the district wasn't based at the main offices. Here they were in a run-down villa near Glienicker Bridge.

I had a chat with the duty officer, enquired about the new processes for inspection measures at border crossing points which were still being bedded in—district Potsdam bordered West Berlin on three sides and the local Department VI was responsible for Schönefeld airport as well as four road crossings, two rail crossings, one waterway and several special crossings not open to civilians. Recently, most of my work had been focussed on tourism and other visitors to the GDR, so it was useful to have a refresher on how systems at the crossing points were currently working in practice.

The comrade from Department VI was keen to make an impression and answered my questions in detail, fetching diagrams and aerial photographs from folders. I let him drone on for a bit, then asked for a register of personnel at a list of local museums frequented by Westerners.

I took the list back to the centre of Potsdam where the main MfS District Administration had their offices on Hegelallee, a huge chunk of chiselled masonry from the time of the Kaisers, and next to it a more homely concrete office block. I headed for the old part of the building, showed my pass and went down to the registry to compare my museum personnel list to the F16 index cards. There was no need to come all the way to Potsdam to check these index cards—we held copies of them in Berlin—but since I was waiting for Lang anyway I might as well use my time, and I hoped that my activities here might be less likely to be noticed than if I'd done the research back at base.

The F16 cards show personal details, as well as which MfS unit first registered that person. Right now I was only interested in names that weren't already in the system, or those associated only with Departments that had nothing to do with their current position in the museums.

I found one virgin, apparently untouched by the hand of the Firm, and a handful who were possibles. I copied out their registry numbers and presented myself to the guard at the next room where I checked the F22 cards, weeding out any that were marked as IM, informant, or looked like they were closely connected to the Ministry. That left me with just half a dozen hopefuls, and I took their accession numbers to the archive.

The whole system is built around paranoid security— the first index card leading to the second index card in a different room where your service roll number is logged for the second time Then with more information from the second card you move to another room where the archive, the actual files themselves, are kept. Without following this chain you have no way of tracing the trail from real name to code name to file.

An hour later, I had a shortlist of four. I jotted down their details and went in search of the canteen.

Digesting my lunch, I wandered down Jägerstrasse to look at the building work. Old ruins were being cleared to make way for new accommodation for colleagues transferring from the capital. Work was coming along nicely, the bosses in Berlin would be pleased.

I turned a couple of corners and skirted piles of rubble that had fallen from collapsing buildings until I found a corner bar. I entered the smoky darkness to wash away the remaining time with a beer or two.

★

At three o'clock, Lang was waiting for me at the Hippodrom, same as this morning. He shook his head when he saw me.

"Nix. Not a single reported missing person in the Königs Wusterhausen area in the last month," he said.

"And the team of technicians?"

"You'll have to give me a day or two if you want it done quietly. If I got the People's Police County Station involved then I'd have preliminary results by this evening."

"I can be patient—don't want word of this getting back to any local state organs."

"Fine." Lang held his hand out, then moved it, tapping his forehead with a forefinger. "Nearly forgot, I've got a contact for you in Königs Wusterhausen *Kriminalpolizei*. Second Lieutenant Strehle will be in the Seven Steps bar near the railway station. You'll find him there from the end of his shift until chucking out time."

"Sounds like my kind of policeman."

Lang ignored my comment, he was checking his watch. "If you leave right now you should make the express."

Lang was right, I was in time to catch the shuttle from Potsdam West and change onto the long-distance service at the Hauptbahnhof. The express had come all the way from West Germany, that much was obvious from the clean and new carriages. The plates on the doors told me it had made the journey from Cologne and was heading for Görlitz, from West to East across two different countries. I sat back in a comfortable seat in a compartment that I had all to myself and lit up a cigarette.

An hour later I climbed down to the platform at Königs Wusterhausen and went in search of the bar. It wasn't hard to find, and I wondered how I'd missed it on my previous visits. It was the usual sort of place, obstinate shadows refusing to yield to fluorescent strip-lights, stained sprelacart tables, hard wooden chairs. Grubby net curtains over the windows sheltered us from the world outside and saved passers-by from having to see us.

My man was obvious, not because nobody wanted to sit near him—all the drinkers at this hour were solitary—it was the military inspired haircut, the clean boots and the straight back. I joined him at his table.

"Captain Lang suggested we meet."

Strehle didn't respond. Not verbally, anyway. He drained his beer and tapped the base of the empty glass on the table. I took the hint and signalled to the barman, who got to work on pulling a couple of beers.

Only after he'd taken a draught of his new beer did Strehle say anything. "Lang didn't say what it is you're after."

I took my time in answering. This was a new relationship and, so far, we'd got off to a good start. No point in rushing in and regretting any false moves later.

"There's a couple of beat policemen I want to talk to," I said.

"Which ones?"

"Niederlehme and Zernsdorf, north of the train station in both cases."

"So go and talk to them." Strehle disappeared into his glass again.

"Unofficial," I told him.

"Unofficial? Well, in that case ..." With a click he put his empty glass on the table.

He was a fast drinker, faster than me. I'd have to take care not to get dragged into his slipstream. I signalled the barman, and asked for a *Korn* to go with fresh beers.

"They'll never know who they're dealing with." I told

him once the beers had been brought over. "I meet them, I talk to them. End of story. No reports."

"Somebody like you doesn't need somebody like me to set up something like that. What do you really want?" Strehle demanded, already making inroads into his beer.

"I have some questions about work morale at the KIM plant. Have you got any informants there?"

"So that's why Lang put you on to me. *Prosit,*" he said, holding his schnapps glass in salute. "What questions?"

Informants are personal. You never talk to somebody else's IM. If you need them to do something or report on something you always go through their handler. It's a special relationship, exclusive, and it needs nurturing. You choose your own potential recruits, you groom them, draw them slowly in until they sign the handwritten declaration, committing themselves to you and to socialism.

At least, that's how we do it in the Ministry, and even if K had the reputation of being lax about handling their own snouts, it still didn't mean I would ever come between an informer and his handler.

I told Strehle what I wanted him to ask his informant, we agreed to meet up again, and in farewell I bought him another glass of beer.

23
BERLIN FRIEDRICHSHAIN

When I got home Renate wanted to talk. I could tell by the way she hovered around as I pulled my boots off and stretched my toes. I ignored her.

I got back from the kitchen, beer bottle in hand and she was still hovering. I switched the television on, and as it warmed up I pushed the neat pile of blankets, sheets and pillows to one side of the sofa and sat myself down. Our Little Sandman had just started his sugary theme tune, and I couldn't help but hum along. The Little Sandman himself was visiting the troops, he had a big bouquet of chrysanthemums for the fighters for peace. As the screen cut to Plumps the water goblin, Renate sat down next to me, a glass of beer in her hand.

"Kid's TV? I didn't know you had a soft side."

I didn't answer, just drank my beer and got bored by the stupid antics on the screen. When the kids started singing the mawkish closing song my wife jumped up and announced she was going to get tea ready. I remained where I was, staring blankly as a presenter told me how to prevent voles digging up my lawn. I didn't even have a balcony, never mind a lawn, so watching it was pretty pointless.

"How was work?" Renate asked through the archway that separated the living room from the kitchen.

I didn't bother answering, pretended to be interested in

an article on potting up anthuriums. Five minutes ago I'd never heard of anthuriums.

"I was hoping I'd bump into you at work, and then I wanted to go shopping, but I wasn't allowed into any of the other buildings. Apparently my pass only gets me into House 18. Should we have lunch together? You could come up to Lichtenberg—the canteen is in my building."

I grunted a non-reply.

"I phoned your extension a few times to see if I could get hold of you, but you never answered."

She was fishing, which pissed me off, but pretending to be interested in pot plants was easier than having an argument.

"In the end I phoned Major Fröhlich to see if he knew where you might be," she said casually as she chopped some parsley.

That did it, she had my attention now. "You phoned the Boss? Well done! What a truly idiotic thing to do. Now he's going to be wondering where I was all day. Thank you very much." I was so pissed off I was practically shouting. I shook my head, then almost under my breath: "Women! Bloody busybodies causing trouble."

That shut her up for a few minutes. I listened to the floral advice and the clatter of the plastic basket of bread slices and the knives being placed on the table, followed by the clink of glasses and side bowls for the salad.

"I'm sorry if I got you into trouble, I didn't mean to," Renate said as she put a plate of sausage down.

I looked over to the table, everything was ready, so I switched the telly off and sat down on the corner bench, pulling my bread board and knife towards me. I'd finished my beer, and Renate put another bottle by my hand, along with the opener.

"I was just so excited to be working at the ministry, I

really liked the idea of lunch with you." Didn't look like Renate was going to give up. That's how she is, when she gets an idea in her head she can't let go.

"Maybe Monday," I offered, as ungraciously as I knew how. Just so long as she didn't get any ideas.

"That'd be nice." She cut a slice of bread in half and spread margarine on it, adding mustard and some chopped parsley on top. "But you didn't say how your day was?"

She wasn't going to give up until I told her something about my day.

"I was grooming a couple of new informants," I used the same excuse that I planned to tell the Boss if he asked, which, thanks to Renate, he probably would. It was bulletproof: I'd write the reports and put in for expenses, and there was no way he could disprove whatever I claimed. But now I'd have to spend half of tomorrow opening fictitious preliminary files on two of my potential sources, detailing my approach, assessing their suitability and potential worth, as well as outlining any plans I had for them.

"Anyone I know?" asked Renate.

"What a fucking stupid question! Even if you knew them I wouldn't tell you, would I?"

"I just thought-"

"Well don't think. There's no way you'd know them anyway, I was in KW!"

Damn, she'd got me to say too much. She was good at that, needling me until I said something I shouldn't.

24
BERLIN JOHANNISTHAL

Renate had a Saturday shift and was already gone by the time I got up the next morning. She had offered to let me back into my own bedroom, but I didn't really fancy sharing a bed with my wife. Not after she'd wound me up so much. Anyway, I had other fish to fry, and today I was going to start preparing the ground.

The first thing I did was give Heidemarie a ring. Luckily, she was at work, which meant I could get hold of her. What's more, she seemed to appreciate my offer of dinner in return for her helping to find the place near Ostkreuz where she and Hofmann had stayed. She said she'd come to Berlin straight after work, and we arranged to meet at half-past five.

But first I had a bit of sleuthing to do. I cleared the dining table and spread out the list of address registrations that Georg had given me on Thursday. It was a thick wad of paper: several hundred Hofmanns and Hoffmanns in Berlin and relatively few Wildes.

According to Heidemarie, Sylvie Hofmann often stayed at her aunt's place in Berlin Johannisthal, and there was no reason not to think the aunt might be harbouring Hofmann now.

I started looking through the lists for Hofmanns and Wildes in that area. I started with her maiden name, Wilde—it was a common name, but not as common as

Hofmann. After that came up negative I started with Hofmann. I had to turn over many pages of Hoffmanns with two Fs, thankful that my Hofmann came only with one F, and that German bureaucracy was efficient enough to keep the distinction in the records clear. As it turned out, I had two Hofmanns who came into question, and a quick look at the map told me they were in those parts of Johannisthal dominated by new build flats.

I walked around the corner to where I'd parked my car, and headed over the river.

As I steered the Trabant under the railway bridge at Schöneweide a tram cut across my path. I slowed down for it, using the opportunity to look to my right where the steps that Heidemarie mentioned come down to street level from the platforms on the bridges above. Further along, I turned into a side road and parked.

The first address I tried was an early slab-built block, five stories high with a pitched roof. I put my finger on the doorbell for Hofmann, and kept it there for a good long while. When there was no immediate answer I pressed it again.

I still had my finger on the button when the front door was hauled open. A short, stout fellow in blue working clothes looked up at me.

"Alright, alright, keep your hair on, I'm here now. The buzzer's broken."

I flashed the K disc at him and he took the involuntary step backwards that everyone does when they realise they have a policeman in front of them. He looked up at me again.

"Citizen Hofmann Werner?"

He was already reaching for his *Ausweis*.

"Do you have anybody staying with you at the

moment?"

He shook his head.

"No relatives of your wife come to visit?"

He looked uncertain for a moment, then shook his head.

"Well? Are there relatives visiting or not?"

"It's just," Werner Hofmann looked at his feet. "My wife died last week."

"Do you have a niece?"

"No, *Wachtmeister,*" He got the rank all wrong, even if he'd only meant it as a mark of respect. "I've no relatives left now."

My second call was just a couple of corners further on. Same kind of building, different kind of person. This time it was a young mother trying to marshal her two children. Her parents didn't live with her, she had no cousins, and no, she wasn't a youthful aunt of any adult nieces.

It was only on the way back to my car that I realised my mistake. If Hofmann had an aunt, whether a sister of one of her parents, or an aunt of her husband, and that aunt had married, she would no longer be using her maiden name, neither Hofmann nor Wilde. I'd have to check back to the parents' generation to get names and addresses and then trace them forwards to the present day. Easy enough under normal circumstances, but once again my investigations were being hampered by the need to stay under the Boss's radar.

There was only one task of any significance to complete that afternoon: find a half-way decent restaurant and arrange a reservation. It didn't take long, bang on the door until one of the waiters decides he's prepared to come and see what the commotion is. Hold the clapper against the class to impress him and when he opens up inform him that I will aceept a reservation for this evening. I briefly thought about trying my hand at getting a reservation at the Cafe Moskau—Heidemarie had mentioned wanting to go there, and if I took her it would impress the knickers off her—but I knew better than to try. The venue was too closely associated with the Party and its functionaries. Attempting to get a reservation, by whatever means, was way above my pay grade.

Still, I was happy with the joint I'd persuaded to host us. A nice little Bulgarian place, and I'd heard good reports about the food.

After that was sorted I went back home and fiddled with the iron for a while. I got my shirt and trousers pressed well enough, my suit jacket didn't need it. I hung them up, gave myself a shower then sprayed on some Western deodorant that had been confiscated at the border and made its way into my possession. I was all set.

I spent the few hours before my date at the Ministry, drafting and backdating prelims to justify my day out in Potsdam. I had to be careful: preliminary files are opened and the proposition is run past the superior officer before any formal approach. Since I hadn't spoken to the Boss about these potential recruits I had to confine my reports to covering fictitious, pre-approach intelligence gathering efforts. It wasn't hard work, I selected two of the four names I'd processed in the Potsdam registry yesterday then built a series of formulas into the report, starting with the political-operational penetration of my area of responsibility, operational surveillance of persons and the development of operational processes (or, in good German: checking out the scene in places Western tourists might end up, keeping an eye open for potential recruits and making a plan to reel them in). The words and phrases I conjured up went on and on about operational this, that and the other. The main thing was that the names I'd chosen were realistic possibles.

There's a little park opposite the entrance to Ostkreuz station, and I waited for Heidemarie next to a bronze, some socialist-realist sculpture of youth. I didn't have flowers or anything, the last thing I wanted was to look too keen. But that's probably how I came across anyway, because when she finally turned up I was checking my watch and calculating how late she was. She gave me an apologetic look as we shook hands.

"Which way?" I asked her. She tilted her head a little, eyes narrowing. "You were going to show me where you and Sylvie Hofmann sometimes stayed."

"Oh! You really ... I thought-" Heidemarie had a hand pressed flat against her breast in a parody of surprise.

"We'll try to find this place, and then go to the restaurant. Deal?"

"Deal." She examined the streets that surrounded the park, her hand still pressed to her bosom. "Things look different in the daylight."

"Let's go back to the station, we can walk out under the railway bridge, as if we'd just got off the train. That might help."

We stood in the shadow of the S-Bahn north-curve as a train thundered overhead and Heidemarie looked around, unsure.

"That way?" she asked, as if it were a test and I knew the answer.

We went that way, and Heidemarie began to look a little more certain of herself. The park was on our left, which made for a pretty good landmark, but when we reached the next crossroads her face fell.

"I'm sorry, I really don't know."

"That's fine. Why don't we come back after our meal—it'll be dark then, and maybe it'll come to you?" I'd reached the conclusion there was no point pushing her, so I took her by the elbow and steered her towards the eatery I'd booked.

We sat in a booth at the back, nice and private. The waiter had done me proud, I'd make a point of blessing this place with my presence again. But right now my attention was on Heidemarie.

She'd had a few glasses of the heavy wine—the same stuff my Boss was quaffing when he broke into my flat a few days ago. She was already a little merry, lubricated enough to be loquacious, sober enough to be lucid. Most of my colleagues have forgotten they shouldn't mix business with pleasure, or perhaps business has become their pleasure. That's not the case with me, which is why I wanted to get business out of the way.

"Any news about Sylvie?"

"Still hasn't turned up. The brigade-leader has started losing it, keeps asking if anyone's seen her."

"You don't seem that bothered? I thought you two were best mates?"

"We were ..." Heidemarie sipped her wine, a red moustache graced her top lip, then she wiped it away with a pointed tongue. "We've grown apart. It's not just that I haven't got much time any more; something changed in her, too."

I topped her wine glass up and waited patiently to hear what she'd thought had changed.

"I've been thinking about it more since you came to my flat. It's kind of like it was her who grew away from me. She was preoccupied all the time, thinking about other stuff. We used to have a laugh at work, but then she got all moony. Do you want to know what I think?"

Why else would I be asking these questions?

"I think she met someone. She's run off with him. Disappeared. How romantic is that?"

"Disappeared?"

"Yes, she'll be shacking up with a hot lover, some cabin in the woods or on an allotment colony."

"What about her husband?"

"Lutz? He'll have to like it or lump it, the way he treats her-"

"Lutz Hofmann has disappeared, too."

Heidemarie put the wine glass down, her back straightened in sudden awareness of how drunk she was. "I don't mean Sylvie's disappeared, not like leaving the country. She and Lutz wouldn't do that ..."

"There are no indications that the Hofmanns have attempted to cross the border illegally."

Heidemarie relaxed again. If the Hofmanns had tried to overcome the border to the West, there would have been serious repercussions on everyone she'd left behind, including friends and workmates.

"So where is she?" Heidemarie asked, peering into her wineglass thoughtfully.

"Perhaps you're right, perhaps she has a lover. But that doesn't explain Lutz Hofmann's disappearance."

"I hope they're not together, she deserves better than him. Way better."

It was obvious she was holding something back, but that was fine. I could be patient. I turned the conversation back to Sylvie Hofmann, wanting to find out more about her character, her background, her social-political attitudes.

But Heidemarie had other ideas, she skilfully steered the topic around to more personal matters. She seemed genuinely interested in detective Ulrich Teichert and I had a hard time keeping my legend straight. The aliases we were given, along with their documentation, were designed to stand up to official scrutiny, but this was a more personal inspection.

I was doing OK, Heidemarie was liking what she saw, she laughed at my witticisms and looked impressed at my stories of detecting criminals. Things were moving along nicely and I was confident enough to begin planning some moves.

The moment came as we stood outside the restaurant. The S-Bahn station was that way, my flat in the other direction. Renate would be there, but I'd just tell her to get out of my bedroom. She wouldn't be happy about it, but that was her problem—I hadn't asked her to come back, had I?

So there we were, standing on the street, just fifteen or twenty centimetres between us.

"I'd like to continue our conversation." I lowered my face halfway towards hers, so close, make it easy to bridge the gap with a kiss.

Her hand fumbled in the space between us, rustling between our coats, and my prick began to pay attention, waking from his slumber. But the fumble was only about finding my hand. Her fingers curled into my palm, her eyes focussed on mine.

"Ulrich," she breathed, her breath prickling my lips and cheeks. "I have to get on home, I have two children waiting for me."

25
BERLIN FRIEDRICHSHAIN

I didn't sleep that night, too busy letting Heidemarie monopolise my thoughts. I wondered why I'd let her get away, and as a consolation, I set my mind to imagining her naked, next to me on the lumpy sofa. But that didn't help me get to sleep, either. I finally dropped off as the sky behind the thin curtains turned grey, but was woken almost immediately by my wife.

"Bastard!" She had a slipper in her hand and was hitting me. I could hardly feel it through the blanket.

"Renate? What are you doing?"

"Coming home, stinking of perfume! Who was she? Who's the slut you're seeing?"

"Nobody, just somebody I was interviewing."

"Do your interrogations in a bar, do you? You stink of wine and ... and *her*!"

I turned over and showed her my back.

"I thought we could make a go of it, try to sort things out." She was crying now, her voice breaking. Any minute now she'd start snivelling.

"Well you've got a funny way of making a go of it, throwing me out of my own bedroom!"

"How can you be so slow, Hans-Peter? Can't see what's right in front of you!" Her voice had receded, and I lifted my head to see where she was. She was in the bedroom, moving in and out of my line of sight through the doorway. I could hear drawers banging, the doors of the cupboard being wrenched open.

I turned back to the wall, best to ride this one out, stay shtum.

"You never change!" Renate was closer again, and I risked a look.

She was schlepping her suitcase towards the flat door, having difficulties manoeuvring it around the furniture. I left her to it.

"Go to hell, Hans-Peter!" I heard her say, just before she twatted the door shut.

26

WOLTERSDORF

After all that excitement I felt I deserved a little pick-me-up. There was no schnapps left, so I made do with a beer. I was pissed off with Renate, not for leaving, but for spoiling the lovely warm feeling I'd had after last night. Now I was thinking about Renate and her unjustified accusations rather than making plans for the further pursuit of Heidemarie.

After the beer I was ready for another snooze, but once again, sleep was difficult to find. I wasn't thinking of Renate any more, which was good, but I wasn't thinking about Heidemarie, either. For some reason my mind had fixated on the problem of Sylvie.

With a sigh I got out of the sack for a second time this morning and went for a piss. Standing over the toilet I thought about Sylvie Hofmann (missing) and the Boss's reaction when I reported the disappearance of Lutz Hofmann (still missing, presumed dead). There was no reason the Boss should be cut up if the husband went AWOL, but he'd totally lost it when I told him. Warned me off in no uncertain terms.

I turned the pieces of information this way and that, looking at them from different angles, and the only way the whole thing made sense was when I included Berg's report of the Boss lugging a body around on the night Lutz Hofmann disappeared. That would be a reason to get ratty whenever Lutz Hofmann was mentioned.

None of this was new, it had been stewing in what passes for my mind for a few days now, and it was getting boring.

"Shit or get off the pot, Reim," I told myself.

Until now I'd been concentrating on Sylvie Hofmann, trying to find out about her, track her down. But Sylvie wasn't the only one at the centre of this sticky web—the Boss was sitting there, right next to her. I didn't know where to find Sylvie, but I damn well knew where the Boss was.

The S-Bahn was empty this Sunday morning and I was the only one to get off at Rahnsdorf. It was one of those middle of nowhere places that Berlin springs on you. No matter how well you know this town, it's always a shock to get off the S-Bahn and find yourself in the middle of the forest. Here I was, only person in sight. A few broken down buildings, the S-Bahn station and an uneven platform for the tram that was at this very moment ruckling its way towards me out of the trees.

When it ground to a halt before me, the driver climbed out. The old fossil took his time about it—he was as dilapidated as his tram. I pulled open the other door and climbed the steps, making myself comfortable on one of the seats. I didn't bother dropping 25 Pfennigs in the box, if anyone challenged me on that they could have a look at my clapperboard.

The driver wheezed up the steps again and pulled the door closed before limping into his cabin. With a few clacks and whirs the tram set off, jangling over points and beginning to sway as it picked up speed over the worn rails. There was no view outside the windows, nothing to look at but endless forest. Some might find that restful, but I'd seen too much greenery this last week and wanted nothing more than to be in the dusty, comfortable streets of the city.

With a resonant rattle the tram pulled out of the forest and into the toy town of Woltersdorf. I pressed the stop button and waited by the door as the wheels juddered us to a halt.

I walked rapidly along the road, back the way the tram had brought me, until I reached the edge of town where I took the track to the left, along the garden walls and fences of the villas that backed onto the forest. I'd only been to the Boss's villa once, a swanky *Jugendstil* residence that he had all to himself and his impeccable wife-and-two-children family. I spotted the turret first, the green copper dome providing a landmark even a factory militiaman couldn't miss. The back garden was screened off by a precast concrete slab wall. It had been whitewashed at some point, but was weathered and grey now, the paint peeling like eczema and wild vine trailing reddening tendrils from the top. I walked along the wall, pulling at the joint lines, peeling off daggers of concrete until I found a slit wide enough to look through.

There was a Hollywood swing directly in front of the fence, but I still had a good view of the garden, and could even see some way into the house courtesy of the glass doors standing open at the back. To my right and built against the other side of the wall was a wooden structure: a garden shed built for a princess.

There was no sign of life, except for the open patio doors. That was enough to encourage me to hang about, at least until I knew whether the boss was home.

I kept my eye to the gap, glancing up and down the path on my side of the wall from time to time to make sure I wasn't surprised by any Sunday walkers. I'd just finished a break—crouching with an eye pasted against a crack is surprisingly tiring—and had begun observing the garden again when a movement in the close right hand sector of the garden caught my attention. I shifted round to get a better angle, and saw a woman come out of the garden house. And not just any woman.

It was my wife.

My operational observation was interrupted when my right wrist was pulled around behind me. Before my assailant could pull my arm up my back I jumped and twisted to my right, pulling away. As I landed, my arm lashed out and I struck the neck of the man opposite me with the blade of my hand, thumb crooked in. Just before the hit landed I clocked his green uniform.

The cop fell away to the side, gasping in pain and surprise, which gave me a moment to assess my situation. I decided against running away, I could probably outrun the officer in his current state, but he'd already had a good look at me, and my Boss would recognise the description immediately.

Holding my left hand up, palm out, I fished the clapper out of my jacket pocket. I flipped it open to the page with my photograph. The cop saw it, his mouth hung open a little further and he stood up again, rubbing his neck and eyeing me warily. Poor sod didn't know what to do. The patch on his sleeve identified him as the local beat officer, so he'd be aware whose garden this was, and now he knew I belonged to the Firm, too. Whatever he did right now was going to upset at least one of the comrades from the Ministry.

"This is an operational procedure," I told the cop, keeping my voice low and hoping it wouldn't carry over the garden wall. "You haven't seen me, nor any other unknown persons in the area. Clear?"

The cop nodded, took another step back, then turned and briskly walked down the path. It was hard to know what he'd do. There was a reasonable chance he had a good relationship with the Boss, and that relationship might weigh more than the implicit threat I posed. I jogged after him, running around in front of him and stopping him again with an outstretched hand.

"Rank and name?" I demanded.

"*Unterleutnant* Kubach, Comrade," he said, standing to attention, but keeping a wary eye on my hands.

Looking at him now, I could see he wasn't as old as I'd thought. Just unfit. "Which police station?"

"Erkner."

"Expect a visit from us sometime next week." I stepped back, and allowed him to continue.

I watched him walk away. By the time he'd reached the next bend he'd looked over his shoulder twice. Good, he was suitably intimidated.

I walked back to the tramline and followed it until I found a telephone box. I put a call through to Potsdam, to Lang at home. He answered on the fourth ring.

"I need an operational team for conspirational observation, plus ancillary operational-technical materiel."

Lang breathed out noisily, letting me know that I was asking a lot.

"Where?"

"Woltersdorf by Berlin."

"Not my region—that's in district Frankfurt." He did the heavy breath thing again. "Ask Strehle, he's closer."

"Phone him, tell him to get here with a team by," I checked my watch, "by 1330. Rahnsdorf S-Bahn station."

Lang didn't reply, and I took his silence as assent.

"One other thing," I said down the silent line. "What

have you got on Strehle?"

"What makes you think I've got anything on him."

"When I mentioned your name, it opened doors. That means you've got something on him. I want to know what." There was no need for the steely voice, Lang knew exactly what I had on him.

"I'll tell you next time I see you. But if you need leverage in the meantime, tell him *Wildau.* Are we quits now?"

I hung up.

As I waited for the tram back to Rahnsdorf I amused myself by wondering what Lang had on his colleague in KW. There are basically three reasons people get into trouble: politics, money and sex. Strehle didn't strike me as the type to raise his head above the parapet for the sake of politics. Which left money or sex. The keyword with which I could hit Strehle over the head was Wildau—a small place, just north of KW. It pretty much consisted of a heavy machinery factory and accommodation for the workforce, which is why I had trouble associating it with sex. That left money. A factory like the People's Own Heavy Machinery Works Wildau "Heinrich Rau" would get through a lot of metal, and some non-ferrous light metals would be worth a Mark or two if they fell off the back of a lorry and straight into the right hands.

It's easy to solve crime when you know the name and the place. The problem is always in finding the proof.

When my back-up arrived, Strehle himself wasn't with them. That was fine by me, all I needed was a deniable surveillance team. I climbed into the lead car and briefed the men on the way to Woltersdorf, providing them with personal descriptions and radio codes for the subjects. Once we'd reached the outskirts of the small town I sent the lead car to observe the front of the Boss's house and I got into the second car to brief them.

I stayed in the second car, a few hundred metres away from the target, out of sight but well within radio range so we could monitor proceedings and, if necessary, take up mobile observation.

We remained in the car for the next three hours, moving into another side road every half hour or so to avoid attracting unnecessary attention. Finally, the radio crackled, then: *Dora on the move. Subject in vehicle accompanied by Paula. Over.*

The driver of my car picked up the microphone, thumbed the transmit button, "Direction?"

Direction north. Am following. Over.

The Boss and my wife were heading towards us, albeit on a parallel road. The driver twisted the ignition, pumping the gas pedal until the engine settled down to a regular rattle, and we slowly made our way to the crossroads with Berliner Strasse.

Main Junction ahead. Subject turning ... The radio gave a crackle, white noise while the pursuit car waited for the Boss to cross or turn off at the junction. *Turning east. Repeat east.*

My driver turned onto Berliner Strasse, the Boss's Skoda was three or four blocks ahead of us, and we passed the first car idling in a side road.

Just before the town centre, the Boss turned left.

"Subject heading north on main road," the driver let the other vehicle know what was happening.

Traffic was light and we allowed some distance between ourselves and the Skoda. We closed the gap as the motorway junction approached and the driver keyed the transmit button again, "Subject possibly going on motorway. Fasan 243 take over."

The Boss went under the motorway bridge, then

signalled right onto the approach road. We throttled back, allowing the other car to take the lead again.

I hadn't expected to be following the Boss onto the motorway, the two teams had been intended for static observation from outside the house, or at most following the Boss for a short walk. But the crew in my car were very professional, they were obviously aware that we needed at least another three or four vehicles to do this job properly, but nobody mentioned it, they just did the best they could.

Just two or three minutes later the radio crackled again. *Subject leaving motorway. Request instructions.*

The driver used the rear-view mirror to look at me.

"Maintain lead position," I told him.

We swapped positions twice on the main road into Berlin, and it was during the second of these manoeuvres, when neither car was particularly close, that the Skoda peeled off to the right without indicating. My driver sped up, but had to stop for a red light. When the light changed, both pursuit cars followed the Skoda's route into the suburbs around Mahlsdorf. I wrestled with a map, trying to fold it so the relevant panels were on top.

"He's probably doubled back around and gone back onto the main road into Berlin, or crossed it and is in this residential area to the south."

The driver turned right twice to check out my theory, but when we got to the junction with the main road I told him to pull over.

I climbed out, thanked the crew for their help and sent them home. There was no point continuing the search, finding a beige Skoda in East Berlin was needle and haystack stuff.

I caught the S-Bahn home, pondering the way the Boss had effortlessly evaded our observation. It told me he'd been aware he was being tailed, which meant the cat and mouse game between us had reached a new level. Only thing was, I wasn't sure who was the cat and who was the mouse.

I arrived at my flat on auto-pilot, but as I reached out with my key I had second thoughts. I turned around and went to the Centre. I didn't understand what the parameters of this game with the boss were, but it looked like it was going to turn nasty for at least one of us. Personally I prefer to avoid nastiness, at least when the stuff is aimed at me, but I was finding it hard to predict what the next few days might bring, and my instinct was to cover my back pre-emptively, rather than after the fact.

I spent the afternoon in the registry, digging up more names to use as cover for time spent away from my desk. This time I concentrated on customs officers—it's harder to find virgins, but you get more brownie points when you do find and turn one.

Dredging through the archives isn't the best way to find potential informants—if I were serious about recruitment, I'd be nosing around the workplaces that were of interest to my department—but the files had the advantage of being the quickest route to finding candidates, and right now I needed quantity, not quality. Anything to show I'd been busy doing my job and not involved in any extracurricular activities.

27
BERLIN TREPTOW

Monday morning at the office was surprisingly mundane. At the very least, I'd expected the Boss to hassle me about Berg, but my presence wasn't demanded on the corridor above. In fact, I think I'd have preferred it if he had put me on the carpet—it might have given me some idea of whether he knew I'd been tailing him the day before. But he left me stewing at my desk, so I made the most of it, trying to cut through some of the bureaucracy that was threatening to choke my filing cabinets.

A circular arrived on my desk after lunch—it was the report I'd written about the Bavarian politician caught dipping his digit in the honeypot last week. I flicked through to see if anything had been changed, initialled the distribution list and took it upstairs for the secretary. When she saw me coming she pressed a button on the intercom.

"Reim is in the office," she said, her voice devoid of interest or sympathy.

She took the file from me and held a hand out towards the door that connected her office with the Boss's. I steeled myself, ready for abuse, but the Boss was working on some files, didn't even look up when I saluted.

"Job for you, Comrade *Unterleutnant*," he announced, signing a chit. Once he'd scrawled his signature, he looked up, face neutral. "Courier job." He flapped the form impatiently.

"Isn't that a job for BdL, Comrade Major?" It wasn't my place to question him, but I don't mind telling you that at that moment I was a little discombobulated—having steeled myself for a temper tantrum, I was faced with nothing more than a menial assignment. "I mean, yes, Comrade Major," I threw in hastily before the Boss could respond to my insubordination.

I clicked the old heels and about-turned, keen to give a respectful impression.

"Remember: courier job, Comrade *Unterleutnant.*" He said to my retreating back.

Don't forget the service weapon, he was saying. Regulations stipulate that a fire arm should be worn on the body when in proximity to adversarial positions, such as on the Border between the GDR and NATO countries, or when personal safety may be an issue and, finally, when on courier service. I usually only wear iron if I'm inspecting a Border Crossing with senior offices in attendance, otherwise the damn thing lives in my office.

I broke the seal on my safe and opened it up, bending down to pull the Walther PP from the bottom shelf. These days, everyone seemed to be wearing Makarovs, but I didn't see any need to hand my ancient handgun in. I fixed the holster around my waist.

Only after I'd put my jacket back on did I read the courier order. Could be worse, just had to pop up to the Centre to fetch something from HVA, the foreign intelligence department.

I was closing my door when the phone rang. It was Renate phoning on an internal line. I put the phone down as soon as I heard her voice.

★

Traffic wasn't too bad and I made it to Ruschestrasse in about twenty minutes. I showed my clapper to the guard on the gate and parked the Trabi. Had to show my clapper again at the entrance to HVA, where they wanted to see my courier order, too. I'd never got further than this, the foreign intelligence department didn't just keep itself to itself, it was a whole, independent organisation within the Firm. Rumour was, not even General Mielke knew everything that was going on in this section.

They kept me kicking my heels for a quarter of an hour or so, then the uniformed guard in the little cubby hole beckoned me over. He dropped a small package on the counter, about as wide as my hand and a bit shorter, maybe a centimetre thick. I checked the seals were in place before signing, dating and timing the receipt, which was then countersigned and stamped. The guard shoved the carbon copy of the receipt at me, then turned his mind to more pressing matters, such as perusing the *Neues Deutschland* newspaper.

I placed the slim parcel on the passenger seat, then put my own copy of *Neues Deutschland* over the top so the guard at the gate wouldn't see and give me hassle for not carrying it in a pouch around my body. But what the heck, I wasn't a courier.

I brought the package to the Boss, who added a third signature to the receipt and handed it back to me. On my way out I passed the receipt to the secretary for filing. As I left her office I glanced through the connecting door, which was still open. The Boss was putting the package in his briefcase.

28

BERLIN FRIEDRICHSHAIN

When I leant back in my chair, I felt the butt of my gun gouge my lower back. It's strange how quickly you get used to something—I don't carry the gun because I don't need to. And because it's uncomfortable having a kilo of pressed metal hanging off your waistband and digging into bits of you every time you sit down or bend over. Yet I'd been at home for what, ten, twenty minutes and still hadn't taken the damn thing off. I unbuckled the holster and put the whole lot in the bedside cabinet. After that I felt light enough to touch the ceiling.

When I floated back into the living room, Renate was standing there, holding shopping bags in front of her. Shield or offering? Hard to tell.

I had nothing to say to her. But before I threw her out I wanted to hear her explanation for why she'd been hanging out with the Boss.

"Perhaps I was a little hasty when I left. I wonder whether I got the wrong end of the stick—and I'd like to make it up to you," she told me.

"How are you going to do that?"

"I thought I'd cook something nice, and we could talk."

Like I said, I was all for listening, but the bit about talking didn't do it for me. The mention of cooking, however ... I put my hand over my stomach, trying to keep it calm. After avoiding the soljanka offered up by the canteen today, my tummy had good reason to get excited at the mention of food.

I sat at the table working out my interrogation approach and watching Renate peel, cut and cook potatoes. If I handled this right I might be able to confirm whether the Boss was aware of the tailing yesterday, and if so, whether he'd seen me in one of the cars. But perhaps more importantly, I wanted to find out what Renate had been up to with the Boss. She'd been at his joint, and that made it personal.

I smoked a cigarette and kept quiet as Renate put the potatoes and dumplings on to cook and got the dishes and cutlery out, and my silence was having the required effect —my wife had stopped her babbling about her new job and was giving me sidelong looks as she laid the table. I was softening her up nicely—she'd soon be ready for me to begin questioning her.

Renate strained the meat dumplings and made a roux sauce from the cooking water. Watching her, I got a bit distracted—she was swaying her hips as she moved from one end of the kitchen to the other, and now it wasn't just my stomach that was getting excited.

The food was soon on the table, and Renate stood to serve.

"Königsberger Klopse," she announced, dishing dumplings and sauce onto my plate.

I speared a few potatoes and added them to my plate and, before Renate had served herself, I cut into the first dumpling and began to eat.

"It's good," I told her, and it wasn't a lie. These dumplings were having the same effect on me as the first sip of beer at the end of a long day.

Renate sat down and started eating, eyeing me over her fork.

"Where were you yesterday?" I asked around a mouthful of potato.

The fork that had been on its way to Renate's mouth paused, then returned to the plate. She got up.

"Beer? Selters?" she asked.

"Yeah, bring a beer."

She returned with my beer and a glass of fizzy water for herself. She sat down and held the glass in front of her, obscuring my view of her mouth.

"Before I answer that, I want to ask you a question," she said.

I stopped chewing. There'd been some kind of misunderstanding—I wasn't here to answer her questions. What could she possibly want to know that was important enough to interrupt me before I even got into the flow?

"When you came home on Saturday night, it was late." Renate was talking again, I hadn't been fast enough to cut her off. "And the next morning you smelled of a woman's perfume. And wine. You never drink wine, so it made me suspicious. Maybe I jumped to the wrong conclusion but —just for my piece of mind—tell me who you were with."

"I can't tell you that, it's to do with work."

"Ah." Renate sighed. She looked down, maybe at the fork resting on her plate. All I could see was the crown of her head.

"I was grooming a potential informer. She's got an operationally relevant position in her workplace and I hope she'll become an IM candidate in the next week or so."

Renate's face raised a little, enough that I could see her eyes peering out from below her fringe. Her red lips formed a perfect O.

"I had to wine and dine her, she's a high level catch." I

was babbling. Why was I making this stuff up. No need to say anything, Renate should just accept what I told her. I watched as she dropped her head a little. I could see tears swimming in her eyes, not yet overflowing, but there all the same. That made me feel a right arse.

"I'm sorry I doubted you. I should have asked before I bailed out on you," she said, trying to smile at me.

I shovelled up another forkful of dumpling and sauce—it was too good to let it go cold.

"Hans-Peter?" Her smile disappeared, and she looked down again. "I have something I should tell you. Last Wednesday, when I came back from Löbau, I didn't come straight here from the station. My first stop was Major Fröhlich."

"Last Wednesday?" I stopped chewing and stared at her. "You went to see the Boss?"

"It's not what you think, honestly. He paid my train fare, arranged it all. Met me at the station and took me to his place. Told me he needed to brief me."

"Brief you?" I was still asking the questions, but it no longer felt like my interrogation.

"I thought he was being nice, I thought he was doing it for you, but ..."

"Renate, tell me!"

"You see, I lost my job in Löbau, had to find another one. Then I got a visit from someone in the district administration, came all the way from Dresden to see me. He said Major Fröhlich was keen that I get back together with you, that the Ministry had to set an example. So I came." She took a sip of water and risked a glance in my direction, then dropped her head again to talk to her still-full plate.

"He asked me round to his, to tidy myself up, I could make more of an entrance, make more of an impression on you if I walked in looking fresh and groomed, he said. I didn't think anything of it, I knew he had a wife and children-"

"Were they there?"

"No. They're on the Baltic coast for a couple of weeks, it was just myself, and-"

"What did he do to you?"

"Nothing, Hans-Peter, I swear. I didn't let him near me. He got the message, and he wasn't pleased. Took me to some flat, where he keeps his fancy woman, told me to make my own way to you when I was ready. So I stayed the night, I was too upset, and came here the next day."

"What's her name? This tart that he's keeping?"

"Sylvie. I don't know her last name." The tears had been released and were dribbling down Renate's cheeks. They looked rather fetching on her, but I had other thoughts on my mind.

"Is that where he took you yesterday?"

Renate looked up, her face stiff. The only thing moving above her neck were the tears, dribbling their way down her face. "How do you know that? You've been watching, haven't you? You've been following me!" She picked up a napkin and dabbed her eyes, then clenched it in a fist, in front of her mouth. "No, not me, your Boss? You think he's up to something, don't you?"

"I think he's been trying it on with my wife!" I tried to recover, but it was too late. It had been a mistake, letting it slip out that I knew where she'd been yesterday.

"Tell me! You know something. It's not just the womanising, it's something else. He's up to no good, I knew it as soon as he picked me up at the station last week."

"So why did you go back to him yesterday?" I demanded, my voice harsh.

"I didn't know where else to go, I was hoping he'd lend me the money to go back to my mother's, but he took me back to Sylvie and told me to think on. He ..." She kneaded the napkin, as if what she wanted to say was stuck inside the cloth and needed help getting out. "He said I was to find out. Stuff. To find out stuff about you."

I fixed her with my cold stare, the one I use when people aren't moving fast enough for my taste.

"Anything you tell me about work, what you get up to, whether you seem odd—anything. I have to report everything about you!"

This might seem over the top to you, all this drama and crying. But remember, I know my wife well, and this isn't how she normally behaves. I'd handled the interrogation badly, but I'd found out what I needed to know, and, what's more, I was now in a position to make Renate my informant and play her back to the Boss.

29
BERLIN TREPTOW

The night interrogating Renate had been a long one, and I spent parts of the morning dozing at my desk. Being able to sleep anywhere is a useful skill to have—if anyone comes in I can be awake in less than a second and looking like I'm hard at work. It does give me a stiff neck though.

After an hour or two my neck had as much as it could take, and I went to the canteen for breakfast. I sat in front of my bread roll replaying last night's conversation with Renate. Thanks to her, I now knew where Sylvie was hiding out, but was still in the dark as to exactly what kind of relationship Sylvie and the Boss had. From what Renate had said, it sounded like the Boss was in control. "She's weak," Renate had told me. "She's as clingy as the underwear the men buy for her in the *Exquisit* shop. But I guess you men prefer women to be like that, don't you?"

My wife held Sylvie in contempt. Maybe it was some kind of jealousy thing. Whatever it was, I didn't see the point of trying to work out what the two women thought of each other, the main thing was that there was no love lost between them. That's why I decided Renate should go and see the Boss's tart again after work. I told her to play nice, stay overnight and do a bit of digging, find out more about the relationship between Sylvie and the Boss.

But my suspicions about the Boss had been solidified by what Renate had told me. I was now pretty certain that the disappearance-slash-murder of Lutz Hofmann was about more than getting Sylvie into bed—the Boss was too clever to do murder just for the sake of a woman. I'd let myself get carried away by simple curiosity and the thrill of chase, but now this case had become a matter of personal and professional pride. I had to uncover exactly what the Boss was up to.

From mid-afternoon onwards I spent a lot of time at the window, keeping an eye on the Boss's Skoda in the car park below. People came in and out of my office with bulletins, circulars, general orders and other kinds of paperwork, and every time they left, I got up to check the window.

At 1843 I watched the Boss get into his car and leave the compound. I headed upstairs with a couple of circulars in my hand, ready to hand them to the secretary if my presence was questioned.

To my mind it was still early, but the brass's corridor had that empty feeling buildings get when nobody's home. The Boss's door had been duly sealed with his *Petschaft*. I made a note of the letter and number combination on the impression in the soft wax, and compared it to my own seal—same design, different number. There was no way into his office for the moment —if I broke the seal on the door then all hell would break loose when it was discovered and the whole department would not rest until the perpetrator had been found and delivered to our prison in Hohenschönhausen.

I left the Clubhouse, and drove randomly for ten minutes or so. Once I decided I'd gone far enough I kept a lookout for a telephone box. When I spotted one I drove round a couple more corners, parked the car and walked back. I put twenty Pfennigs in the slot, waited for the red light and put a call through to Strehle. There was no answer at home, and I considered calling his work number, but decided I didn't want the KW police switchboard logging the call. It was nearly seven in the evening, and I had a pretty good idea where I could find him.

Forty minutes later I was pushing open the door of the Seven Steps bar in KW. Strehle was in the same corner I'd left him on Friday, and he didn't bother looking up from his beer as I sat down opposite him.

"Thanks for organising the observation teams," I offered.

"Thanks for the beer," he replied.

He was a simple man to please. I caught the barman's attention, but he was already skimming the foam off two glasses of pilsner. A moment later they were on the table.

"That doesn't cover your bill, mind." Strehle said, in place of a toast.

"Way I see it, the bill you owe society still needs paying off."

He didn't respond, and we both drank deep from our glasses.

"You want more, don't you?" Strehle finally looked up from his beer. His face was red, and his pupils contracted only slowly as his eyes tried to focus on my face.

"Wildau," I tried out the magic word.

He thought about that for a bit, then came up with a question. "Is that a threat or a request?"

"Just a little bit of metal work I need doing."

"That so?"

"Listen, Strehle, I look after my own. You help me out, when the time comes I'll help you out."

"And how do you propose to do that?"

127

"The way I see it, your little game in Wildau is going to get busted. Sooner or later, it's got to happen." I didn't need to know exactly what he was doing in Wildau to bullshit him about it. "When the lid gets blown off it, well, that would be a really good time to have your name in the records as being on the side of socialism."

"You're saying I should be your informant?"

"You give us a report every so often, I file it and my lot have all the incentive they need to give you protection."

Strehle sipped his beer. Then he sparked up and decided to keep an eye on the ceiling. Maybe it had started spinning already.

I got up and asked the barman for a candle and a piece of paper. Once he'd passed them over I took them into the toilets. I locked myself in a cubicle, put the seat down and laid the piece of paper flat on it.

I struck a match and lit the candle. When it had melted a little, I dripped wax onto the paper, in a rough circle, and quickly pressed my *Petschaft* seal into the wax.

Blowing out the candle and putting my seal away, I took out my penknife and carefully cut away all but the first of the numbers embossed on the wax. That hid my own identity, but still showed the size and style of the numbers stamped in the centre of the seal. I tilted the paper to the light, checking the quality of the impression. It wasn't quite clear, but good enough. Finally I wrote down the number of the Boss's *Petschaft* and folded the piece of paper.

I brought Strehle a glass of *Doppelkorn* schnapps and set it down in front of him, along with the piece of paper.

"Do we have a deal then?" I asked him.

"You even in the right department?"

"In my line of work there's no such thing as the wrong department."

"What do you need?"

"This." I slid the piece of paper closer to him. "I need it copied, but with the number I've written down.

Strehle lifted the flap of paper slightly, enough to peer inside, but not enough that anyone else in the bar could see what he was looking it. His face grew pale as his eyes followed the letters around the circumference: *Ministerium für Staatssicherheit.*

"Damn. You don't ask for much, do you?" he growled, his eyes back on the ceiling. "This is way heavier than anything in Wildau."

He wasn't wrong. Forging a *Petschaft* is probably the worst crime you can commit in the GDR, don't let anyone tell you otherwise. Fleeing the Republic or spying for foreign agencies is nothing compared to this level of disloyalty to the bureaucrats who run the Republic.

"Can your friends do it?" I asked after Strehle had had the beer he needed to regain his composure.

"Shouldn't be a problem. Cut off a piece of aluminium bar, punch the letters and numbers in, solder a knob on the back. Easy enough. But you'll have to give them a bit of time if you want it looking just right."

"Tomorrow then?" I asked.

Strehle pushed the paper away, shaking his head. "This is serious stuff."

"You got any other options right now?" I used my friendly voice. No need to scare the man, he could work it out for himself.

"Tomorrow, then." Strehle downed his schnapps.

30
RANGSDORFER LAKE

In the departmental briefing this morning I reported on my successes in the preparation of potential sources. The Boss looked pleased, while others in my section were less gracious. I asked for an appointment with the Boss to discuss the creation of a file on my latest potential in Königs Wusterhausen, and he agreed readily, suggesting we talk immediately after the briefing.

Once the colleagues had filed out of the conference room, I made my case for preparing to recruit Strehle as a candidate source for the department. No names were mentioned, naturally, but I had prepared a strong case: experienced police officer in the criminal investigation department in a county responsible for a border crossing into West Berlin, not to mention the respective hinterlands of Schönefeld airport and a further border crossing used by West Berlin rubbish lorries. The subject had approached me from a sense of duty and responsibility towards society and the state. He had produced low-level intelligence in the past, and while useful, it had not been of such operational significance that he'd been noticed by the District Administration's Line VI. I argued that the source could be positioned to produce operational information that we could pass along to the Central Co-ordination Group responsible for attempts to flee the Republic.

"Has this potential source come to your attention ancillary to operations you are currently involved in or aware of?" the Boss asked. He was talking in subtext: *is there a link to the job I gave you to do, and if so, what the hell were you doing talking to the local Volkspolizei when I told you to keep it low-key?*

"No, Comrade Major," I answered. "I became aware of the person with the assistance of a colleague at the County Administration of the MfS. He was unable to prepare the person due to operative restrictions." Subtext: *I was owed a favour.*

The Boss seemed satisfied. On the surface it was all fine. Strehle's credentials were good, and he'd be useful to the Department. Only when you looked at the man himself did you realise quite how unsuitable he was as a source. I could only hope his cadre files didn't mention his drink problem or his lack of discipline.

"Permission to create a file on this person, Comrade Major?" I asked. The Boss nodded assent, so I continued. "I'd like to continue my observation and examination of the person today with a view to expediting the recruitment process."

The Boss glanced around the room, as if checking nobody else was present, then leaned forward. "Don't you think you've been spending enough time down there?" he hissed.

"Yes, Comrade Major. That's the reason I want to open a file. Explains my presence." I leant forward and lowered my voice, too. "It also gives me cover for dealing with that last operative difficulty."

"No," the Boss gave me a hard look, wondering what I was up to. "Let things cool off a bit, first. Why don't you follow up those other persons you're developing?"

"The ones in Potsdam?" Potsdam was a good fifty

kilometres away from KW, in the Boss's mind that was probably a safe distance.

"In Potsdam," he confirmed.

Back in my office I opened the road atlas and, using my finger, traced the two possible routes from East Berlin to Potsdam. I needed a place on the way to Potsdam, but not too far for Strehle to travel. It also had to be after the Schönefeld motorway interchange—which had cameras and a watchtower—so if the Boss was in the mood for checking he could see I'd been a good boy and had made my way to Potsdam without delay.

In the end, I settled on Rangsdorfer Lake, just south of Blankenfelde. Satisfied with the choice, I left the Clubhouse in my car. I followed the usual procedure when using a phone box—a quick and dirty dry-clean—before putting the call through.

I'd been waiting half an hour or so when Strehle turned up in a shabby Wartburg Kombi with rust around the wheel arches.

"There's a hotel around here somewhere, bar might be open," he suggested.

I pulled him in the other direction, into the woods between the village and the motorway.

We followed a path that went up a slow hill, or what passes for a hill in these parts of the Republic, and Strehle was soon out of breath. When we reached the top I offered him my hip-flask to reconcile him to missing out on the bar at the lakeside below. He swigged greedily, then pulled a face when he realised it was a sweet herb liqueur.

"More kick in a bottle of Club-Cola," he complained, but took another nip before handing the flask back.

The trees that surrounded us were in a poor condition, the pine needles were either brown or completely absent. But the diseased trees weren't struggling, because in Real Existing Socialism, acid rain does not exist. Whether or not the needles were officially dropping, the naked branches allowed us a good view on all sides. We'd be aware of any other walkers before they were within hearing distance.

"Your friends working on the thing?" I asked.

"It'll be ready as agreed." Strehle was kicking through the drifts of brown needles. He'd discovered a bunch of brown mushrooms, nibbles taken out of them by some unknown creature.

"Have you spoken to your source at the chicken factory?"

"I've got some news for you. Heidemarie Müller, associate of Sylvie Hofmann? Short version: thick as thieves, the pair of them. Müller, two children, estranged from husband since he put in for permission to leave the Republic. Despite this she managed to get herself accepted as a candidate member of the Party. Obviously that didn't last, not with her husband in the background, estranged or not. She managed to keep a lid on it, but when another Party member reported seeing her with her husband the Works Party Organisation ended her candidature-"

"When?"

"Seventeenth of last month."

Which meant that since before I'd got to know her, Heidemarie had no longer been a Party candidate, despite all her talk about how dedicated she was and how much Party meetings and schoolings were taking her away from her children and her best friend.

"Any idea why she's been meeting up with her

husband? Does he have access rights to the kids?"

"He comes round to the flat on a regular basis. We suspect they're not estranged, just pretending to be because they think it will give him a better chance of getting an exit visa."

"Does she want to follow him to the West with the children?"

"Hard to say. I think if anyone knows, it would be her colleague, Sylvie Hofmann, the one you asked about. Like I said, thick as thieves. Spend lunch breaks together, leave work together. Best mates. Or were, until last week, since which time Hofmann hasn't been seen. Do you want me to keep the observation going?"

"No, put it on hold for the time being." I turned to go back down the hill, but Strehle put his hand on my arm.

"I've got something else for you," he said.

I half-turned, body angled toward him, feet still pointing downhill. I was impatient to get going, wanted to think about what Strehle had told me, and what it meant for my investigation, as well as for my personal life.

"You also asked about missing persons. Müller Sylvie isn't the only one. Although, he's not really missing, more of a fresh corpse."

"Who?"

"Fellow by the name of Dieter Berg. Of the white ribbon persuasion."

Shit. Berg, dead? I kept my face straight. "Cause of death? Time and place?"

"Thought he might be on your radar. Can I have another go of your flask?" Strehle took a swig and screwed up his face. "According to the Murder Investigation Committee a blunt trauma to the back of the head was the likely cause of death. The body was found at

2025. No signs of rigor, rectal temperature had fallen by less than one degree."

"Stop flirting. Time of death? Where? Who found him?"

"Best guess: around 1930, plus-minus twenty minutes. Reported by a traffic cop who took exception to Berg's Trabant being parked by the side of the road through the Tiergarten. When he stopped to investigate he saw a citizen with a dog which was behaving oddly, sniffing and pawing at freshly turned earth. The traffic cop called in colleagues from K and they found the body, twenty or thirty metres away from the road, by the side of a path."

"In the woods?"

Strehle emptied the flask, then nodded.

I turned away from Strehle and looked through the naked pines to the sky beyond.

I had nothing to do in Potsdam other than show my face at the District Administration. I went to the main building on Hegelallee and fetched a pile of random but authentic-looking files, then sat at the reading desk, thinking about what Strehle had told me.

Berg was dead. No clues, no witnesses, but the timescale fitted. Yesterday, the Boss had left the Clubhouse at 1843. Add half an hour to get to KW, which put his arrival there at a quarter past seven in the evening. A quarter of an hour later, Berg was dead.

But why? The Boss had ordered me to ensure Berg's silence. Maybe he no longer trusted me to do the job, in which case, how many more bodies would turn up?

Or maybe it wasn't the Boss, just a coincidence?

I wanted to know more, but I needed to be very careful. Berg was an exiteer, which meant his death would automatically be considered a political matter. And murders with political aspects usually got taken over by the colleagues in Main Department IX. Once they started asking around, someone would remember that Berg and I had met a few times. I'd been to his workplace twice, his exiteer pals might have seen me that night in Treptow— I'd hardly been discreet. I'd relied on the fake cop ID to keep my interest in Berg compartmentalised from my day job.

That meant I was safe enough while it was just cops asking questions—there was no link they could follow between me and the paper personality of *Obermeister* Teichert of K. But the Firm's Department IX Special Commission were a different matter. Once they got involved my cover wouldn't last half an hour.

31

BERLIN TREPTOW

After a quick meal in the Potsdam canteen, I made my way back to Berlin, this time along the trunk roads rather than the motorway. I drove as far as Adlershof, a couple of S-Bahn stops south of Schöneweide, and found a place to park in a residential street. I checked my watch for what was probably the tenth time since leaving Potsdam, time was tight, but I should make it.

I caught the tram to Köpenick, a suburb of Berlin with a village feel to it. More importantly to me right now, it was a place where several bus and tram lines converged. Once there, I jumped on the first bus that left, sitting near the front and keeping my eyes open for a bus coming the other way. When I saw one approaching along the straight length of Müggelheimer Damm I changed on to it and went back to Köpenick. Once there, I headed into a department store, came back out through another exit and managed to get on the tram number 86 just as the doors were closing.

My final rinse was on the S-Bahn—back one stop towards Berlin, then across the platform to get on the S-Bahn heading to Königs Wusterhausen.

I considered repeating my hygiene procedure once I got to KW, but I didn't have the time. Anyway I'd never felt more alone in my life. So after snorting a brief beer in the station bar, I caught the 1508 S-Bahn back towards Berlin.

It was timed to serve the early shift as they left the Wildau works. I sat in the first carriage, second bench on the right hand side, and was very careful not to pay much attention to my surroundings when we pulled into Wildau station. I didn't look at the serried brick-gothic factory halls to the left of the tracks, nor at the matching housing blocks to the right. I didn't glance around when a worker sat himself next to me. And I paid no attention at all when he left the train, particularly not to the fact that he'd forgotten to take his copy of the *Märkische Volksstimme* newspaper, folded up on the seat between us.

In fact I ignored the newspaper all the way to Adlershof, at which point I casually picked it up and took it with me when I got off. I could feel the hardness at the centre of the newspaper, but kept it clamped under my arm as I climbed into my car. I didn't unwrap it until I reached my office.

The newspaper was flat on my desk, the counterfeit seal lying on top. I placed my own *Petschaft* next to it, and compared the lettering. Whoever had worked the plate had done an excellent job. I was pleased with Strehle's connections.

My admiration was interrupted by a knock on the door. I folded the paper back over the aluminium stamp and swept it into a drawer. "*Herein*," I mumbled.

It was another circular, eyes only, and the courier waited while I scanned the documents and initialled the distribution. Once he'd left, I decided to get on with some real work. I'd be here for a few more hours yet.

The Boss's Skoda wasn't in the car park today, but enough other *Bonzen* had their cars there for me to estimate the population of their corridor. I kept my eye on the Ladas, Wartburgs, Chaikas and the lonely Volvo. One by one they slipped their moorings and when the last had sailed into the night I went on a reconnaissance tour of the upper corridor. Every door was sealed, the only sound was the clack of my shoes on terrazzo tiling. I returned to my office, left the door ajar, and waited for the night duty to do his rounds.

I had the desk light on when I heard the clicking of uniform boots. A shadow slipped through the gap between door and jamb, and once it had slid by, I peered out to watch the sentry reach the stairwell and slowly descend to the floor below.

That was it, I had at least half an hour, more likely up to two hours before the Boss's corridor would be patrolled again.

I pulled the counterfeit *Petschaft* out of my top drawer and made my way upstairs. I didn't creep around, but nor did I stamp my way down the corridor. Discreet, but looking like I belonged—that was my aim. I pushed through the doors at the top of the stairs, and when I got to the Boss's office, I pulled the thread that connected the seals on his door. I managed to get the cord out without too much damage to the surface of the wax. In the dim lights of the corridor nobody would see that the seal was broken unless they were actually checking. Satisfied with the results, I got to work with the key picks. One by one I pushed the tumblers out of the way and smoothly turned the torsion key until the lock clicked. Depress the handle, and I was in.

My first move was to the window. I drew the curtains then went back to the door. I took off my jacket and laid it on the floor at the bottom of the door, and only then did I turn the light on.

The Boss's office was like any other in the building.

Worn brown lino that smelt of polish and *Wofasept* disinfectant. A mix of pre-war and prefab furniture and the obligatory portrait of General Mielke overseeing it all.

I had four main targets in the office: desk and side table with typewriter, safe, clothes hanging on the coat rack and wall unit cupboard. I decided to start with the clothes. The Boss had left his everyday uniform on a hanger, and I patted the pockets: spare change, a spent match and a receipt from a *Delikat* shop.

Next up was the desk. I checked the typewriter on the side table, no paper in the platen, nothing underneath. I then mentally divided the desktop into six, memorising the positions of each object in the first section before moving anything in my search, then replacing everything and moving onto the next section. It was overkill, because there was nothing of note on the desk. The telephone (nothing underneath), the blotter (ditto), empty filing trays (ditto).

The drawers of the desk were locked, but none were sealed, which told me there was no official material kept there. I picked the lock to check anyway. Personal items: a *Ruhla* fob watch, coloured pencils, a pen with a broken nib, empty forms. I slid the drawers to and picked the lock again to close it.

Moving to the cupboard, I found the Boss's dress uniform (pockets empty) and boots along with some clean shirts folded up on the shelves. I hadn't expected to find much in the places I'd searched so far, nevertheless the lack of anything personal or official was disheartening.

The final target was the safe. It was a metal cupboard with a key lock and a wax and cord seal, just like the door to the office. I got to work on the lock, and every time the torsion key slipped the whole safe made a pinging sound, it reverberated like a metal drum. The lock finally gave,

140

and I pulled on the metal door which broke one of the wax seals. The door shuddered open, scraping loudly over the sill. I paused, door in hand to stop it swinging, face turned to the office door. I must have waited for a hundred, maybe two hundred seconds, and on hearing nothing but my own breathing, turned back to the safe.

Top shelf left: more shirts. Top shelf right: the Boss's side arm and ammunition.

Middle shelf left: files, stored flat, about ten centimetres worth. Desk diary on top. Middle shelf right: empty.

Bottom shelf left: two pairs of shoes to match everyday uniform or civilian clothes. Bottom shelf right: a grey archive box, containing a full bottle of vodka and two glasses.

I took the files and desk diary over to a clear corner of the desk and flicked through the diary. There were two types of entries: times written next to the standard short code for individual officers, indicating official meetings. The second kind of entry was in a different kind of code. One or two letters, times, sometimes further short codes that suggested places. I checked the Friday before last, the day Lutz Hofmann had gone missing. After 1600 there were no entries. Before that time, a list of official meetings. Paging forward to look at yesterday's entry, I wasn't surprised to see the same pattern—entries only for work appointments during the day and nothing after 1830.

I flicked backwards through the diary, hoping to find lots of meetings with S for Sylvie or H for Hofmann. Nothing.

I put the diary to one side and started on the files, checking each page. All were boring: minutes of past meetings, agendas of upcoming meetings, circulars—the kind of stuff that snows into my office every day. The kind of stuff that the Boss must have had left over at the end of the day and had just shoved into the safe to deal with tomorrow.

I rearranged the files so they were in their original order and put them back into the safe with the diary on top and locked up. I picked out the mass of wax on the safe door, moulded it into a flat coin, then pressed first the cord, then the counterfeit *Petschaft* into it, making a seal.

I sat down in the Boss's chair, seeing the world from his position for the first time.

It didn't cheer me any.

My left hand was on the armrest of the chair, my right hand was on the desk. Looking at my left hand, I had an idea. I allowed it to drop, mimicking a gesture I'd observed in this very place a couple of days before. My hand loosened as it moved down, as if depositing a package into a briefcase standing open on the floor.

I knelt down and looked underneath the desk. A grey A4 envelope lay there, as if it had been carelessly dropped into the briefcase, but had missed and floated out of sight. I pulled the envelope towards me, and still on my knees, took out the single sheet of paper inside and quickly scanned it.

It was a passage order for the border crossing point Friedrichstrasse station, with a couple of blanks still to be filled in. *The holders of the personal identity documents issued by the independent political entity of Westberlin and bearing the numbers .... and .... and with ultra-violet activated security marks to the left of the date of birth are to be permitted to exit the GDR without let or hindrance. The bearers of the above named identity documents are not to be questioned or searched but are to be assisted in any way requested. All members of the Pass and Control Unit and the Customs Organisation of the GDR at the Border*

Crossing Point Friedrichstrasse Station are to be informed of these arrangements which are in force for a period of twenty-four hours after issue of this order.

This was the kind of order we handed down when foreign intelligence were inserting operatives into the operational area of West Berlin. The instructions would come from HVA, and we'd type up something appropriate and dispatch it off to the relevant border post.

So far, so normal.

But in the top right hand corner was a code: HA VI/6/HPR. The code identified the person who had drawn up the order. That was the person who would be held responsible for any consequences that came of following the order.

Funny thing was, it was my personal code.

32
BERLIN TREPTOW

When a case throws a sledgehammer at you, you just have to dodge it. If you try to catch it, you'll end up dropping it. You drop it, it lands on your toes and that's you out of action.

This was going to be a hard one to dodge. The Boss had pinned a target the size of West Berlin on my back. I was pretty sure the package I'd couriered a few days ago contained the personal identification documents to be used with the order—the size and weight seemed about right. I'd signed a receipt when I picked them up, and handed a copy to the Boss's secretary for filing. If the Boss had subsequently removed the receipt copy from the files it would look like I'd never handed over the package. By murdering Berg, the Boss had ensured that Department IX would get involved—and it would take them less than a day to follow the kilometre-wide trail that led to me. And when they got to me they'd discover the trick with the missing receipt for the West Berlin ID docs and the passage orders that had my personal code on, even though I had no authority to issue them.

It was a neat plan, and sitting here in the Boss's chair, I couldn't see any holes in it. The Boss was heading West with his bimbo, and he was leaving me to face the music.

If I had to quibble, I'd suggest the Boss's plan relied on tight timing—he needed to issue the passage orders and cross over into West Berlin before Department IX took the murder investigation off the local K. I held the orders in my hand, the Boss hadn't filled in the serial numbers of the ID documents yet, so it looked like he wasn't expecting immediate action from IX.

Without thinking too much about the risks, I switched on the Boss's electric typewriter and fed a sheet of paper into the roller. I copied out the passage order, making sure to reproduce the spacing as closely as I could. I wound the piece of paper out of the typewriter and checked it against the original. There were two barely noticeable but very crucial differences—I'd shortened the originating code to HA VI/6 so the orders would no longer be attributable to myself, and the new version had been typed on the Boss's typewriter. That was a nice bit of insurance: if they ever came to check which machine had been used to type up the orders, the finger would point firmly at the Boss.

I put the new orders into the envelope, placed it back in its original position under the desk and took the old orders with me.

I took my time making sure I'd left no traces in the office—unplug the typewriter, sweep the desk and side table for hairs, check position of everything I'd touched. Turn the light off, open the curtains, leave the room, reseal the door.

The first thing I did when I got back to my office was light up and get the office bottle out of my safe. After I'd reacquainted myself with my two best friends, I had a closer look at the original passage orders I'd taken from the Boss's office. I scrutinised the typeface, and I may not be one of those experts, but the lower case h was faint, and the n tailed a smudge more often than not. I pulled out one of those preliminary reports I'd been working on and checked the typeface there.

The passage order had been written on my typewriter. The Boss had been in my office and typed up his passage orders right here in this chair. I wasn't the only one with a dodgy *Petschaft*.

33
BERLIN TREPTOW

The duty officer had a store of camp beds for those who needed to remain on duty overnight, but rather than draw attention to the fact that I was still at the Clubhouse, I laid myself out on the floor behind my desk, using my jacket as a pillow.

At 0713 the next morning I phoned Medical Services at the Centre and asked to speak to my wife. I was told she'd call me back.

Nine minutes later, my phone rang, and I asked Renate if she wished to have breakfast with me. She didn't answer immediately, down the line I could hear her thinking.

"I'll be there in twenty minutes," I told her and hung up.

Seventeen minutes after that, I was driving through the checkpoint at the gate on Ruschestrasse. Another four minutes and I was sitting in the canteen, a cup of coffee in front of me, checking my watch and waiting for Renate to appear.

She came in through the door, looked around the tables until her eyes met mine, then hurried over.

"You'll never guess-"

"Renate," I interrupted. "Shut up. Let's go for a walk." I took her by the elbow and steered her towards the exit. Renate's pass was only valid for entry to and exit from the compound via the Normannenstrasse entrance, so we left that way and turned left.

Still with my arm on her elbow, squeezing hard whenever Renate opened her mouth to talk, I walked her to the end of Normannenstrasse and crossed the main road, taking her into the Stadtpark. We passed the amphitheatre and walked under the spare canopy of the pine trees until we reached the open meadow that ran along the western edge of the park, next to the railway marshalling yards. I found a bench where we could see anyone approaching from a good forty or fifty metres away.

Renate was keen to talk, so I let her speak without prompting or questioning.

"Sylvie Hofmann is such a gossip! I don't know what your boss sees in her."

I nodded to show I was listening, even though I was continuously surveilling the park.

"She told me she's leaving the country-"

"Any destination mentioned?" I interrupted.

"She didn't say. She was talking about somewhere sunny, the Crimea, Sochi perhaps. And she says she's going with a friend."

"A friend?" And the friend wasn't the Boss—Renate had used the female form, *Freundin*.

"Yes, her *Freundin* is arriving today, and they're leaving tonight. Got the tickets and everything."

"Name? Does this *Freundin* have a name?"

"Heide, she called her. Or Heidi? Something like that."

She meant Heidemarie. But was Heidemarie really prepared to leave her kids behind? Did she have a plan that involved her husband fleeing over the border with the children? It didn't add up.

"Anything else?" I asked, but Renate was already

venting about thankless citizens leaving the Republic, despite all society has done for them.

I ignored my wife's political complaints and tried to work out what this new information about the *Freundin* meant. If I was wrong in my assumption about the Boss leaving with Sylvie then I'd have to come up with a whole new plan of action.

"Renate, shut up for a minute, just listen. Go back to work, tell them you're ill, you have to go home. But don't go home, go straight to the station and take the train to your mother's. Stay there until I tell you it's safe to return to Berlin."

"Safe to return? Hans-Peter, you're being ridiculous-"

"Do as I say!"

"And anyway," Renate continued talking, as if I hadn't just snapped at her. "I don't even look ill-"

"There's a *Konsum* down the road, get some black pepper. Breathe in a handful before you go and see your superior."

"Now you're being silly. Anyway, what if there's no pepper in stock?"

"Renate! By telling you to stay with Hofmann I've put you in danger—she's going to be arrested soon, and I don't want you anywhere near her when that happens."

"Arrested? How do they know?"

"They don't. At the moment only you, I and the Boss know. Now will you get on that train to Löbau?"

"But Hans-Peter-"

"Trust me on this, please. I want you out of Berlin on the next train!"

Renate nodded, her eyes fixed on the gravel path before us.

34

BERLIN TREPTOW

After meeting Renate in the park, I went back to the Clubhouse and asked the secretary for an appointment with the Boss.

"You've just missed him," she informed me.

When I asked whether he could fit me in that afternoon, or maybe the next day, she fetched his diary out of the drawer. She riffled through, settled on today's date, then hurriedly turned the page, but not before I saw all the entries scored out.

If for a moment I'd believed Sylvie's guff about leaving with a female *Freundin*, I certainly didn't any more.

"Day after tomorrow?" the secretary asked, flicking forward another page.

I agreed an appointment I knew we'd never keep and left the building.

"First of all, I want to meet the Murder and Investigation Committee." I told Strehle down the telephone line. I was in a phone box somewhere off Baumschulenweg. "Tell them I'll meet them the day after tomorrow with all the information and the proof they need to close the case. If I haven't contacted you by the end of tomorrow then you can also tell them to widen the search in the Tiergarten— they'll find at least one more body." I was setting up my life insurance—the kind that only pays out if you fail to make it home one day.

"I've got a feeling I shouldn't ask you how you know this?"

"And I need another favour from you," I said, ignoring the question.

"I hope it's an easy one this time." Strehle sighed. I was making him work hard for the scant protection I was offering.

"Same as Sunday."

"Same subject?" he asked.

"Same subject, same location. Have them phone me at my office once a specific direction or possible destination has been identified. And I want another team in Mahlsdorf. Subject inexperienced, one team should do." I gave Strehle the address of the conspirational flat where the Boss had parked Sylvie Hofmann then hung up and returned to the Clubhouse by a roundabout route.

Now I sat at my desk, waiting for Strehle's surveillance team to phone me with news. I could have joined the operational observation team outside the Boss's villa in Woltersdorf, but I preferred to remain static until the other pieces started to make their way across the board. Here I could plan my own moves and wait in comfort for situation reports.

The Boss must have spent months preparing the paperwork to justify a mission for two operatives in the Operational Area of West Berlin. But now I was thinking about it more, I saw that the strength of his plan was also its weakness. His position in the Firm meant he'd been able to get his hands on real or forged West Berlin identification papers, and he had the authority to make sure the documents were accepted at the border. But the same apparatus that allowed him to do all this also gave me the ability to stop him with just one phone call.

It was a question of timing. If I called the border post too soon the Boss could countermand my stop order. If I prevented him from crossing into West Berlin, he'd be in a position to make sure I looked like the villain thanks to the massive target he'd pasted on my back. He'd be stuck here with his girlfriend, his wife and his kids, but he wouldn't have to answer for his law and marriage breaking.

A knock at the door interrupted my thoughts. At my command, an NCO marched in, presented a document and left again.

I put the document in the safe to deal with another day, and since it was open, I reached into the bottom shelf for my service weapon.

It wasn't there.

I knelt down, feeling around at the back of the shelf.

Nothing.

I cast my mind back, when did I last see it? I'd carried it when fetching the package for the Boss on Monday, and had left it at home that night—it would still be in my bedside cabinet. I considered going to the quartermaster for another weapon, but the explanations and the forms would mean spending at least an hour away from the phone. Going home would cost nearly that much time as well, but I had to stay here, waiting for the phone call from Strehle's teams. There was no choice but to go without.

I waited impatiently by the phone, picking holes in the blotter on my desk and wearing out the lino under the window.

When the phone rang I grabbed the receiver so hard that the phone slid across the table and, with a jangle of the bell, hit the floor.

"Hello? Hello!"

The line whirred, then a voice, faint and fading, then growing in strength.

"Subject Berta on S-Bahn travelling towards centre."

"I'll take up radio contact in ten minutes," I told the telephone and hung up.

I hastened out of the building, then slowed my steps to a less conspicuous pace. I walked to my Trabi, relieved to finally be on the move.

At the top of Kynast Bridge, next to Ostkreuz station and the highest point for miles around, I pulled over to the side and switched on the radio, nudging the dial round until I had the frequency used by cops in the Potsdam district.

"Konrad Eins, come in," I said into the microphone, ignoring the cars that were coming up behind me and beeping.

Konrad Eins receiving. Over.

"What is your present position, over?"

Mühlenstrasse, heading west. Over.

I pulled back into the traffic, tires swishing through the puddles, and took the sharp turn down the ramp onto Rummelsburger Hauptstrasse. Turn right, under the railway bridge and back towards the river. Once I'd reached the Osthafen I took the mike again and thumbed the transmission.

"Konrad Eins, present position? Over."

Holzmarkt, near Jannowitzbrücke.

"Location of subject Berta?"

S-Bahn heading west. Next station: Marx-Engels-Platz.

I put my foot down, weaving through traffic, chancing the gaps in the oncoming vehicles. A W50 truck honked at me as it slewed to its right, sending up a spray of dirty water as it lurched through a pothole. A Wartburg on the far side of the road braked sharply to avoid being crushed by the swerving truck. I ignored the chaos, nudged the wipers up to full and edged between two Trabants on my side of the road.

I eased the pressure on the accelerator, and the screaming of the engine subsided to a high whine. The thrum of wet tires deepened.

"Konrad Eins, update?"

Subject at Friedrichstrasse station.

I was at least ten minutes away, and Hofmann was about to get off the S-Bahn and disappear into the crowds of central Berlin. I pulled into the middle of the road again, jerking the steering wheel around another pothole, playing chicken with oncoming cars.

Subject Berta on foot heading north, the radio crackled at me, just audible over the rattling bodywork. *Konrad Zwo and Konrad Drei following on foot.*

I was nearing the Red Rathaus, traffic was thickening and slowing. Instead of fighting my way through the mess of vehicles, I did a U-turn in the middle of the road, driving the few hundred metres back to Jannowitzbrücke station. Grabbing the radio set and abandoning my Trabi in a no-parking zone, I ran up the steps to the platforms. An S-Bahn was pulling in and I dragged on the handles even before it came to a stop, pulling the doors open, and pushing against the press of bodies leaving the train. I stood just inside, sweat and rain mingling on my forehead, all eyes in the carriage looking to the left of me, above me, out the window by my side—everywhere but at me.

Subject Berta heading west, Reinhardtstrasse.

The eyes around me flickered as the radio said its piece, but quickly returned to their careful non-scrutiny. The bell rang and the red lights glowed as the doors wheezed shut. The S-Bahn gathered speed, snaking along the viaduct, too slow, insisting on stopping at Marx-Engels-Platz before finally pulling into Friedrichstrasse station.

I was pulling on the door even before it was released, the hydraulic resistance no match for the adrenaline coursing into my muscles. I jumped down, angling forwards to reduce the deceleration as I hit the platform. The bulky radio on its strap swung around as I half-stumbled, half-ran towards the steps down into the guts of the station. As I approached the doors onto the street I lifted the mike.

"Konrad, location?"

The radio clicked as I released the transmit button, but there was no answer. I broke into a trot as soon as I was outside and joined the stream of pedestrians on Friedrich-strasse. As I ran over the bridge that took the street over the River Spree, I thumbed transmit again, the button slick with moisture.

"Konrad, location?" I repeated, panting as my breath failed me.

Contact with Subject Berta lost.

My strides shortened, my feet slowed, and I came to a halt, bending over, hands on thighs, struggling to breathe.

The radio buzzed and the mizzle hissed off my hot neck.

We've lost her, over.

35

BERLIN MITTE

I clipped the microphone back on the radio and pulled the strap from my shoulder to tuck the unit under my raincoat. Reinhardtstrasse was just a few metres away, and as I entered the street, the skyline was taken over by the impossible mass of the concrete air raid shelter that stood at the first junction along.

Before the bunker, outside the agricultural publishers, a grey Zhiguli stood, its wing jutting out into the carriageway to give the driver a clear view down the road. I crossed the street and walked down the pavement until I got to the car and climbed into the back seat.

"Where did you lose her?" I asked, trying to keep my voice steady.

"Just here, Comrade," the driver answered, his face pointed forward.

Over his shoulder, I could see a man standing point further down the road. He could have been one of the willing helpers from Sunday, who knew? These cops all looked the same.

"Talk me through it."

"I stopped immediately before Friedrichstrasse railway bridge to allow Konrad Drei to join Konrad Zwo in pursuit of Subject Berta on foot. I followed in the vehicle, remaining in visual contact with the designated points man at all times. When I was outside the Interhotel Adria the points man indicated a left turn-"

"Who was point at that moment?"

"Konrad Zwo, Comrade. By the time I had reached the junction and waited for a break in the traffic, Konrad Drei had returned."

"Konrad Drei was the one who lost contact?" I looked down the street. It was straight, a clear view all the way to the railway bridge.

I took the radio from under my coat and laid it on the seat. It was too bulky—not only did it slow me down, it made me too conspicuous.

"That Konrad Drei standing right there?" I waited for the driver to nod. "Right, give me your gun."

"Comrade?" The driver still had both hands on the steering wheel.

I shoved my hand between the two front seats, just within his field of vision.

The driver reached under his left armpit, pulled out his *Wumme* and placed it in my hand.

Standard issue Makarov. I checked the safety, pulled back the slide and ejected the magazine to count the bullets. All in order. I double checked the safety and put it in my jacket pocket.

I climbed out of the car and went to see Konrad Drei, standing patiently in the rain.

"You lost the subject," I told him when I got near.

"Yes, Comrade." He'd been aware of me coming but had maintained observation of both Konrad Zwo, who was a further fifty metres down the road, and the car, fifty metres behind us.

"Tell me."

"Subject left Friedrichstrasse station on foot and proceeded along Friedrichstrasse, direction north then along this street, direction west. Subject remained on the left-hand side. I followed on foot, on the right-hand pavement. A convoy of NVA personnel carriers came from direction west, and at the same time, a tourist bus came from direction east." He took a moment to break eye contact with the Konrads, just long enough to wave a hand at the narrow street. Cars were parked along our side, there was barely room for the wide trucks to pass, even if a bus hadn't been coming the other way.

I could see the problem. If you follow a subject with just one vehicle and two on foot then the subject doesn't need to have experience in counter-surveillance to lose you. They just need a bit of luck.

I dismissed the Konrad, told him to return to KW and take his pals with him. Standing at the junction again, I watched the three of them drive off.

I slowly turned around, looking down each of the roads that joined the crossroads. There were four immediate routes that could be taken, and within a hundred yards there was also a car park and a further three roads.

Not to mention dozens of buildings she could have entered. I was looking north, along the side of the bunker, towards the Deutsches Theater, when I heard the rumble of a four-stroke engine beside me. It was the cops from KW again. The driver rolled down his window.

"We've just received radio contact from Ludwig Eins," the other team, which I'd set to watching the Boss's villa. "Subject Anton is in a civilian registered UAZ-469, current location Strausberger Platz, direction Alexanderplatz. Thought you should know, Comrade."

"How many cars are following?" I asked.

"Two following and one ahead of subject."

It was still too few teams to tag an experienced operative, but was better than the situation we'd had on Sunday—the UAZ jeep was a much slower beast than the

Skoda, which would make it harder for the Boss to shake a tail off. What's more, I finally had another piece of evidence connecting the Boss to the disappearance of Lutz Hofmann—Berg had reported seeing the Boss in a Russian jeep, and in the dark, any UAZ would look like a Soviet Army vehicle.

"Go and join the tail." I opened the door of the car, and pulled my radio from the back seat. "With four cars you can do a basic box. Stay in contact."

I took my raincoat off and slung the radio over my shoulder, then put the coat back on over the top. The boxy receiver hung at my hip, sticking out of the bottom of the coat. I clipped the microphone to the strap, under my coat, but still easy to reach, then looked around for somewhere to position myself. There was nowhere at ground level with a good view of the whole area, but the windows of the tenement opposite overlooked the junction.

I crossed the road and pushed open the door to the hallway, then went up to the second floor. There were two flats at the front of the house, and I knocked on the nearest door. There was no answer, so I moved on to the second door.

I'd given up waiting and was about to get the picks out when the door shuddered open. A veteran, half my size and three times my age peered out. I showed her my K disc and pushed past her. That didn't seem to bother the old dear, but she did tut to herself when I opened the window and sat myself on the sill. I ignored the pensioner and took stock of the cars below, noting positions and colours, memorising blocks of shapes rather than individual vehicles.

There were few pedestrians on the street, the rain was doing its bit by keeping everyone indoors. Anyone who was out didn't look up. This was a good vantage point and I was unlikely to be seen.

I was still doing my initial visual sweep when the radio crackled.

Konrad Eins in position. Location subject Anton Weinmeisterstrasse.

The Boss was getting closer.

My checks were interrupted again, this time by the biddy.

"A cup of coffee?" she asked, holding her hands in front of her belly.

I didn't bother answering, just continued watching the flow of traffic below. In this position, my blind spot was traffic heading north on Albrechtstrasse. Persons or vehicles travelling in that direction would appear without notice, and if they turned left I wouldn't be able to get a good look at them. I concentrated on that corner, scanning the other three roads every few seconds.

Anton leaving vehicle Oranienburgerstrasse junction Linienstrasse. Proceeding on foot direction west.

He was close, so very close.

Anton approaching Permanent Representative of the Federal Republic.

The Boss was heading towards the West German mission—was he about to defect? I snorted, it was involuntary—before last week the suggestion would have been absurd, but now? Now anything felt possible.

Anton has passed Permanent Representative ... Entering building Humboldt University, section Veterinary Medicine, staircase B ... Ludwig Drei burnt repeat burnt.

He'd made one of his pursuers—which meant not only were we a man down, but the Boss was now aware he was being followed.

Ludwig Fünf taking up pursuit, Anton exiting at rear.

The Boss was just north of me, but between us was a network of park-like gardens divided by walls and hedges with a thousand doors in a hundred buildings. He was going for a dry-cleaning run.

Anton proceeding direction west, correction east entering building 25.

Another voice took over the reporting. *Ludwig Drei, Anton steps to cellar, in pursuit,* but the message fizzled into white noise, then, with a static click, fell silent as the radio signal disappeared into the cellar.

Box building 25 repeat box building 25.

I recognised the voice of Konrad Eins ordering the teams to surround the building the Boss had entered, but then Ludwig Drei came back on air.

Ludwig Drei. Anton in connecting corridor to adjacent building proceeding direction south.

Move box, Konrad Eins ordered. *Include building south of 25.*

Ludwig Drei contact lost repeat contact lost.

Ludwig Drei had lost sight of the Boss.

Konrad Eins to Ludwig Drei, maintain position connecting corridor. Konrad Eins to all other units: cover exits 25 and adjacent buildings.

But my helpers from KW were too late, they were surrounding a building the Boss was no longer in, he was too good for them.

I left the window and ran into the kitchen where the veteran was washing up.

"The university gardens—where's the nearest entrance?"

She turned around, holding onto the side of the sink to steady herself. When she'd managed a full hundred and eighty degrees, she fumbled for the glasses hanging from her neck on a piece of string. I wanted to grab her and shake her, but knew that would slow things down even more.

"The university gardens? The Humboldt University?" she asked, peering at me through the glasses.

"Nearest entrance? Where?"

"Go down the side of the orange store," she whispered, drawing back a pace.

"Orange store, what's that? Tell me where!"

"The old bunker, the air raid shelter left over from the war."

I was already halfway down the stairs.

I ran across the road and along the front of the bunker. At the other side a brown, oil-slicked stream stank its way along a ditch, skirted by a dirt track, more mud and puddle than track. At the back of the bunker a gate barred the way, I didn't bother checking to see if it was locked, just vaulted over and into the gardens. The grass was thin, barely covering muddy patches slick with rain. Trees dotted the area, obscuring paths and buildings, but I stayed by the stream, heading north, towards the area where the Boss had last been seen. A large building, built in the same brick-gothic works as the factory halls in Wildau, angled towards the brook, narrowing the garden as it converged with a villa in front of me. That provided a pinch point which the Boss would have to go through if he was heading towards Friedrichstrasse station.

Or he could take one of the other two routes I could think of off the top of my head.

I positioned myself beside an old lime tree, the trunk wide enough to give me cover. From here I could observe the pinch point, as well as the doors leading out of the back of the building next to me.

"One in three chance," I muttered. "One in three."

The tree trickled grimy rain over me, it ran down my forehead until it got lost in my eyebrows. Every time a drip landed on me I blinked, and every time I blinked, I imagined the Boss had got past me in that split second.

It was after one of those blinks that I saw her. Sylvie Hofmann was sashaying down the path by the stream, like a chorus girl from the old Friedrichstadt-Palast stepping out for a breath of fresh air between rehearsals. She nimbly stepped around puddles, handbag over one shoulder, a brown umbrella held above her head.

I edged around the tree trunk to remain out of sight until she was past me, gave her a fifty metre head start, then followed her, staying on the sticky grass to dampen the sound of my steps.

I was back in play.

36

BERLIN MITTE – REICHSBAHNBUNKER

Following Hofmann was easy—she didn't look around, she didn't double back or dart into buildings without warning. Even if she had turned around and seen me she wouldn't recognise me. But I did keep a wary eye open for the Boss, he was still at loose somewhere nearby.

Hofmann was already passing the rear of the Yugoslav embassy, cutting across the range of the bulky cameras mounted on the wall above. Shortly after that she did a sharp right, at the nearest corner of the bunker. As she turned, she looked back the way she'd come, towards me. I can't swear to this, but I'm sure she gave me a half-smile as she did so.

I hurried up to where she'd disappeared, no longer worried about getting my feet wet in puddles. When I got there, I took a sly peek around the corner. A wire fence with a gate in it. On the other side, concrete slab paving, buckled and cracked from the weight of trucks, led to the road at the far end. No Hofmann.

The gate wasn't locked, and I let myself through, gauging distances as I went. If Hofmann had run fast she may have made the street at the far end of the bunker. I hurried along the concrete track, not hanging around, but slow enough to make sure I didn't miss anything that

might be out of place. And there it was: the side of the
bunker had been cut open at this point, enough of it had
been hacked out to make room to allow the back end of a
W50 in. The gap was closed off with two steel gates, and
one was standing ajar. Just a couple of centimetres, but I
spotted it.

I stepped around a puddle that took up most of the
mouth of the bunker and put my ear to the open door.
Damp air tickled the side of my face, and I could hear a
tapping echo, a high clacking, two beats. Footsteps.
Women's shoes with a narrow heel striking the concrete
floor.

The door was heavy but well balanced, it opened easily.
Inside was dark, and a damp but sharp and fruity smell
forced its way up my nose. Coming in from the autumn
rain, the space before me was noticeably a few degrees
cooler.

I edged around the door and into the dank blackness.
Feeling my way along a wall I went in far enough that the
light through the open door no longer backlit me, and
waited. Back and hands pressed against rough concrete,
listening and letting my eyes adjust.

The double-beat of footsteps had stopped, but now I
caught a hollow thump, a zip opening, a repetitive rustle
of items being shifted around. Everyday sounds of
someone rootling through a bag, but oversized—stretched,
bent and echoed by the acoustics of the bunker. Although
the sounds reached my left ear they were stronger and
purer from the right and I turned in that direction.

There was a click, and the room splashed with light. As
my pupils adjusted, my brain registered the source as a
weak torch beam, surprisingly bright after the absolute
darkness of a moment before. It played against a surface
just around the corner from where I was standing,

sweeping me into darkness, then returning me to reflected half-light.

From the way the shadows played, the greyness of reflected luminosity and the areas of solid blackness, I worked out I was in a room or chamber, blast protection wall opposite me, narrow doorway opening into a corridor to my right. On my left the room remained in darkness, its dimensions unknowable.

I felt my way forward, my toes making first contact on each step. At the doorway, my hand grasped for the solidity of the wall, but found none. I pressed my arm against the darkness, fingers extended until they made contact with concrete, twenty or thirty centimetres further away than the shadows had suggested.

Millimetre by millimetre I broke cover, peering for the source of the light which was already receding around the next corner. To my right, familiar darkness hid unknown dangers. Ahead of me, the torch beam filtered through a doorway and played off a close wall. I could hear the footsteps again, growing fainter as the light dimmed. More sure of the evenness of the floor now, I followed the last glimmer through the door, doing the zombie thing with arms outstretched, feet rapidly scuffing the ground. Another two twists, the way shown by the merest suggestion of torchlight, and the twin-echo of the footsteps changed to a more regular staccato. Stairs.

A left turn, the rhythm of feet on steps had ceased, and the scattered second-hand light no longer touched the ceilings, just the floor at the bottom of a staircase. As I made my way to the steps the light withdrew and disappeared and all I was left to focus on was the vague memory of the glow at the top of the stairs. I went up, sticking close to the side, my hand shading the dull effervescence of the phosphor stripe painted along the walls.

By the time I made the top of the stairs there was no light at all. I sidled over to one side, and stood in the darkness, listening.

There was no footfall, no click, no forewarning before light poured through the whole level of the bunker, leaving me exposed at the top of the stairs. I blinked in the harshness of the glare coming from a caged lightbulb above, and quickly swept the room I was in. My back was against the concrete wall, but the other sides of this chamber were hidden behind heavy wooden shelves filled with crates. My eyes flicked across the stencilled labels: NARANJAS CUBANAS, then concentrated on the doorways. I edged towards the nearest gap, still relying on ears rather than eyes for guidance and straining to pick up the echo of footsteps, the same narrow heel tacking against the poured concrete floor.

I made better progress now I could see, pausing only at each doorway to check for moving shadows before risking entry to the next room.

I found her after two more rooms and three more turns. She had a crate half pulled out, and was helping herself to a wizened green orange.

"Hello," Hofmann said without turning towards me. "I was hoping you might join us."

"Where's Fröhlich?"

"Have you been looking for these?" Hofmann pulled a fat envelope out of her handbag. The package that I had brought to the Boss from foreign intelligence a few days ago. She held it out, inviting me to take it.

Confused, I took a step forward, then another, my arm lifting towards her, hand opening to receive the unexpected gift.

"Hold it right there, Reim." The voice was behind me,

but it echoed off the walls and shelves, making it seem like the Boss had surrounded me.

I turned my head, and the Boss was kind enough to move so I could see him more easily. He had a pistol in his hand, and it was pointed straight at me.

Hofmann was grinning, the package in her hand still available. When I turned my head to see the Boss again, he'd shifted back out of sight.

"Kneel down," he ordered.

I got down on my knees, stretching my arms to the sides, aware of the heavy tread of the Boss's shoes as he came closer. He shoved me hard on the back of my head, and I collapsed forward, my arms breaking my fall before my nose could. With a hand pressed on my head, and a knee on my back, the Boss first spread my arms out, then patted me down, removing the Konrad's Makarov from my coat pocket.

"This isn't your weapon—you're one of those nostalgia freaks still toting the PP, aren't you?"

I didn't reply, the way the Boss screwed his knee into my spine told me he wasn't looking for answers.

"So where's your service weapon, Comrade Second Lieutenant?" he mocked. "What about regulations?" He stood up, then placed a foot between my shoulder blades, pressing me into the cement. I had my head turned to one side so my nose and lips didn't have to suck dust.

"Bring me the ID cards, Sylvie," the Boss said, his voice almost kind, the tone slightly off, as if he still needed some practice in being affectionate.

Hofmann danced two steps towards us then darted off to the side.

"Sylvie," there was gravel in the Boss's voice now, making it sound a lot more familiar. "Not the time for piss-"

He never finished the sentence—there was a burst of noise that echoed around the chamber, making my eyes sparkle, and the Boss was lying on top of me, his mouth pressed into my ear. His lips were wet, they dripped warm liquid onto my face.

Pleasant as it was, lying in a bunker with the Boss on top of me, I didn't hang around. I rolled to the right, pitching my superior's body off as I went. My hand reached out for his shooter but came up with nothing. I didn't fancy dawdling long enough for a good look so I jumped up and ran to a corner where the shadows cast by the underpowered light bulb were a little deeper.

Only then did I check my surroundings. Only then did I see my wife, a familiar looking Walther PP trained on me. She stood professionally, one hip dropped, feet placed perfectly, arm outstretched, pistol barrel pointed in the same direction as her eyes: straight at my chest.

"Open up the package, Sylvie." Renate said without moving her gaze from me.

I didn't take my eyes off Renate either, I could hear the brown paper being ripped, could hear the flap of cardboard booklets being opened.

"They're blank," Sylvie said in a different voice from the one she'd used on the Boss. It was raised in excitement, but it was firm, not breathy-flirty.

"Right, Reim," Renate said, for the first-time ever not using my hateful forenames. "This is what's going to happen. You're going to take those identity cards, and you're going to go to wherever it is you have to go for the right printer or typewriter or whatever you use. Then you're going to put our names on them, and you're going to put those rivets through our photos. We've got the rubber stamps here, so we'll do that bit."

"Our names? Us?" I asked. I had a feeling that my

mouth might be hanging open. I reached up and shut it, then threw a look at Sylvie who was on some kind of adrenaline high, laughing.

"Idiot! Different names. Women's names."

"You two?" Only then did I realise. "I'm not going to do that. I won't help you flee the Republic."

"Reim, don't be an arsehole all your life—look what happens to arseholes." She flicked the pistol towards the Boss's carcass.

"If you shoot me then I can't print up the ID cards. You need me."

"Shit Reim, only arseholes argue when someone's pointing a gun at them. Sylvie, can you do this, I've already had to put up with enough idiocy from him over the years."

Sylvie joined Renate, standing directly in front of me.

"Renate tells me you're a bastard. She said the first thing you did when she returned was slam her face into the wall—your toerag boss blackmails her into coming back to Berlin and all you can do is-"

"Blackmail? The Boss was blackmailing you?" I was looking at Renate now, needing an explanation.

"Your boss forced me to return." Renate sighed. "I didn't just lose my job in Löbau, your boss made them sack me. Then he sent me a message, said I wouldn't get another job in Löbau and that if I stayed anyway he'd make sure I was prosecuted for not working." She looked at my gormless mug and frowned in irritation. "He wanted to sleep with me, you idiot. That's all."

"Did you?"

"Right now I'm tempted to kneecap you. Sylvie?"

"Reim, it's simple." Sylvie put on a bored face. "Your boss has set you up to be the fall guy-"

"I know he framed me, I'm not stupid!"

170

Sylvie ignored the interruption. "You're as pig-headed as your boss, Reim. Do you think he came up with this idea all by himself?"

Was the bitch telling me this was all her idea? If that pistol wasn't pointed at me ...

"And your ex-wife has just shot your boss with your weapon which she found in your flat," Sylvie continued. "So if you don't co-operate, we'll tie you up and leave you here, and tomorrow morning, when you're found, your colleagues from the Firm will have a lot of questions for you. Like why you were attempting to leave the country, like why you shot your boss-"

"I get it already!" I yelled.

Sylvie tutted, Renate didn't react.

"Renate tells me you're a low-flier, so I'll make this simple for you. Look over there." She pointed towards the doorway, where a briefcase stood on the floor. "Fröhlich's. In there is the receipt for the ID cards you couriered, and the pass orders you oh-so-*cleverly* changed, along with another set of the original orders, typed on your typewriter and with your code at the top. You help us, we leave you the courier receipt and the pass order that was typed on your machine. Any questions?"

"What about the body?"

"He's as bad as Fröhlich," she said to Renate. Then, to me: "Do you expect us to work everything out for you?" Sylvie rolled her eyes. "Can't you deal with anything by yourself—I don't know, dig the bullet out and dispose of it, dispose of the whole damn body. What do we care?"

The two women looked at each other and laughed.

37

BERLIN FRIEDRICHSTRASSE

The ID cards were quickly typed up with the names Sylvie and Renate had given me—all I had to do was take my bloodstained coat off, find a sink to wash the Boss's blood off my hands and face and walk out of the bunker and around the corner to the nearest police station. I showed them my K disc and demanded the use of a room and a typewriter.

I left the ID cards on a shelf just inside the door of the bunker, and walked down Friedrichstrasse to the exit hall at the border crossing point. I used the side entrance, and went to see the officer in charge. He was senior in rank to me, but I was from the Centre, so he took the passage order without quibble.

I remained at the crossing point, sitting before the bank of video cameras, waiting for Sylvie and Renate to present themselves. Half an hour later, the camera outside picked them up as they showed their new West Berlin ID to the policeman standing at the door. The internal cameras showed them at the top of the steps that lead down into the exit hall. As they joined the end of the queue for the customs check, I made eye contact with the young *Feldwebel*, pointed to the two women on the screen and sent him off with a message for customs.

The *Feldwebel* appeared on my monitors, standing behind a customs officer who was taking apart a suitcase.

The customs officer nodded as the *Feldwebel* whispered in his ear.

Sylvie was next, and I watched as her suitcase was opened, the customs officer's hands only lightly passing over the clothes inside before the suitcase was shut again. He turned his attention to Renate's luggage. Same procedure.

The two women waited patiently in the queue to go into the passport control cabins. Renate went first, I could see her on the camera positioned above the confined space in which travellers are expected to stand while their documents are checked. She held herself erect and I could detect the pride in her stance. I watched as she passed her ID card through the hole. This would probably be the last time I ever saw her. Good riddance.

Sylvie Hofmann was next, and once the door had shut her in the cabin, I went down to see her. I sent the border guard out and sat in his chair, looking through the glass at the woman I'd been hunting for the last week. She stared back at me, doing a good job of hiding her nervousness. It went against all my training to sit here and allow her and my wife to flee the Republic. But they had power over me. For the first time ever, I realised my wife had power over me.

"Why did you kill Lutz Hofmann?" I asked Sylvie.

"He deserved it. Five years of hell he put me through, so I got your boss to get rid of him. Not that your boss was any better. You all deserve it, every single one of you."

I pressed the release button, the buzzer sounded and the door to the cabin swung open on Renate and Sylvie's new life in the West.

First Chapter of
OPERATION OSKAR
the sequel to Stasi Vice

"Where were you between 1600 and 2200 hours on the night of the fifteenth?

My comrades love a good question, maybe that's why they were asking me again. And again.

And again.

OK, I know what you're thinking. Why didn't I just answer?

But I'd already answered. I'd given them my answer this morning. And yesterday. And the day before.

And guess what? They were still keen to hear what I had to say.

I knew the procedure, I knew what to expect—I'd been on the other side of that table many times. I'd heard the lectures at the Ministry school in Golm and I'd read the manual. But this time I was in the hot seat. Knees closed tighter than a nun's, hands pressed under my thighs, palms pushed against the seat. No sleep for two days. Or was it three? Couldn't really tell whether the hallucinations were from alcohol withdrawal or lack of sleep.

Probably both.

So I gave them my answer again: "I was in my office, opening a preliminary file on a potential informant in Potsdam. The gate records will confirm that I spent the whole night at the headquarters of Main Department VI in Treptow."

The Stasi major sitting behind the desk didn't react. Didn't even bother looking up from the sheet of questions in front of him, just read out the next one from his list.

I didn't need a sheet of paper in front of me, I knew which question was next because he'd already asked me, as had the interrogator before him, and the one before that.

Like I said, they love a good question.

The shifts changed. The faces opposite me changed. But I stayed right where I was, and that list of questions stayed right there on the desk.

Every day or so they let me go back to shiver in my cell, just for a bit of variety. My cramped legs struggled to carry me down the cold corridors, my hands were shackled together and my head was lowered.

I couldn't see much. The traffic light system was above my line of sight, my vision topped out at the thin wires strung along the walls at shoulder height.

I thought about reaching out, pulling the fine wire before my guard could react. Break the electrical connection and the alarm would go off, more screws would turn up, truncheons ready for action. Surely the pain and the bruises would be better than this monotony?

Just for a bit of variety.

They were having a hard time deciding whether my dead Boss was a hero or a traitor and they expected me to help them work it all out.

Everyone else who could help was either dead or in the West. Either way, they were out of reach.

Fair enough, it was going to take them a bit of time to figure it out: all they had was the Boss's corpse with a big hole in the chest where a bullet had been dug out of it. They didn't know who had killed him.

But that wasn't the important bit.

They wanted the *why*. If they knew why he'd been killed they'd know whether he was a class-hero or a class-traitor.

Once the brass agreed on the why they might declare him a hero—just for the propaganda value—even if they'd decided he was a traitor.

Or it might happen the other way round. Who could say how it might turn out?

And me? I couldn't care less whether my dead Boss was a hero or a traitor. I only cared what the comrades thought. The interrogation notes would be sent to Berlin Centre, and one day the verdict would come back.

If the bigwigs decided the Boss was one of the bad guys then I was as good as dead.

LIST OF MAIN CHARACTERS

Members of the armed organs (MfS, DVP)
Holger **Fritsch**, captain, HA XX.

Major Roland **Fröhlich**, Reim's immediate superior when he was posted to HA VI.

Hauptmann **Lang**, DVP Potsdam.

Erich **Mielke**, general. Minister for State Security.

Hans-Peter **Reim**, second lieutenant, HA VI.

Polizei Unterleutnant **Strehle**, *Kripo* Königs Wusterhausen.

Other characters
Dieter **Berg**, engineer, applied to leave the GDR.

Frau **Dittmann**, sales assistant, Konsum.

Sylvie **Hofmann**, switchboard operator, KIM.

Lutz **Hofmann**, worker at concrete plant. Sylvie's husband

Heidemarie **Müller**, switchboard operator, KIM. Ex-wife of Heiko **Müller**, who applied to leave the GDR.

Renate Vera **Reim**, nee Kubzyk, Reim's wife.

Marco **Westhäuser** - lorry driver for VEB Likörfabrik. Lives opposite the Hofmanns.

GLOSSARY

MfS units

Abteilung – Department. The **Hauptabteilungen** (HA—main departments) were based in Berlin (most at Berlin Centre in Lichtenberg), responsible for national co-ordination and strategy in their areas of responsibility.

The *Abteilungen* were sub-departments of the HAs, either based in Berlin, (e.g. Abt. M, Abt. 26) or the equivalent departments in the *District Administrations*and *County Offices*. Most local departments kept the number of the Main Department they belonged to (e.g. Abt. II represented HA II), the main exception being Abt. XV, the local level of the HV A.

Main Departments were further divided into Sections.

Bezirksverwaltung des MfS, BV – District Administration. Each of the 15 administrative districts in the GDR had a MfS District Administration, which co-ordinated operations in that area. The next administrative level down, the counties (*Kreise*), had offices in each county town (**Kreisdienststelle, KD**).

Department see *Abteilung*.

Bezirksverwaltung des MfS, BV – District Administration. Each of the 15 administrative districts in the GDR had a MfS Administration, which co-ordinated operations in that area. The next administrative level down, the counties (*Kreise*), had offices in each county town (**Kreisdienststelle, KD**).

HA, Hauptabteilung – see *Abteilung*, or the specific Main Departments below.

HA VI – Main Department VI, passport control, tourism, transit traffic, where Reim was posted until autumn 1983.

HA IX – Main Department IX, investigation, interrogation and prosecution of suspects.

HA XX – Main Department XX, state organs and institutions, culture, church, underground groups; security of military communications infrastructure.

Kreisdienststelle, KD – see *Bezirksverwaltung*.

Main Department – see *Abteilung*.

Ranks (DVP, MfS, NVA etc)

Feldwebel – sergeant, staff sergeant.

Hauptmann – captain.

Hauptwachtmeister – police sergeant.

Leutnant – lieutenant.

Major – major.

Unteroffizier, Uffzi – the lowest rank of the non-commissioned officers (equivalent to corporal / sergeant), also generally used to cover all NCO ranks.

Unterleutnant – second lieutenant.

Wachtmeister – police constable (corporal).

GDR/German/other terms

Ausweis – identity card. **Personalausweis** was the civilian identity card, **Dienstausweis**, service identity (eg for work or in the armed organs, including the military **Wehrdienstausweis**). These Ausweise were little booklets, most with a cardboard and/or plasticised cover.

ABV, Abschnittsbevollmächtigter – beat policeman with responsibility for a particular neighbourhood or area.

Berlin Centre – MfS headquarters in Lichtenberg, Berlin. Also known as *Stasi Zentrale, Ruschestraße* and*Normannenstraße*.

Bonze – bigwig, (mil.) brass, party leaders.

Botanik – greenery, leafy suburbs. Berlin dialect.

Centrum – department stores run by the *HO*.

Clubhouse – Reim's term for the HA VI headquarters in Treptow.

Clapperboard – Reim's term for the MfS ID document, commonly called *Klappfix*.

Comrade, Genosse – member of the Socialist Unity Party (Communist party of the GDR), member of the army and other armed organs of the GDR.

District see *Bezirk*.

Doppelkorn – grain spirit, schnapps.

Exquisit – expensive boutiques that sold limited edition, GDR produced fashion items not available in the usual shops.

Federal Republic of Germany; FRG, Bundesrepublik Deutschland, BRD – West Germany

GDR, German Democratic Republic; Deutsche Demokratische Republik, DDR – East Germany.

GÜST, Grenzübergangsstelle – border crossing point.

Havarie – technical breakdown, disaster, write-off.

Herein! – come in! Enter!

Hohenschönhausen – borough in Berlin, location of MfS central remand and interrogation prison **UHA I**.

IM, Inoffizieller Mitarbeiter – unofficial collaborator of the MfS.

Interhotel – chain of international standard hotels in the GDR.

Jugendstil – German equivalent of Art Nouveau.

Kaufhalle – self-service supermarket.

KIM, Kombinat Industrielle Mast – combine of feedlots / factory farms.

Kneipe – pub, bar.

Kohlroulade – cabbage wrapped around meat.

Kombinat – vertically and horizontally integrated industrial group.

Konsum – one of the two main retail organisations, a consumer co-operative.

Kripo, Kriminalpolizei, 'K' – Criminal Police, the criminal investigation agency for police forces in German speaking countries. The abbreviation *K* was unique to the GDR.

Ministerium für Staatssicherheit, MfS, Stasi – Ministry for State Security, secret police and intelligence agency.

Neues Deutschland – national newspaper in the GDR, central organ of the *SED*.

Nordhäuser Doppelkorn – schnapps from Nordhausen distillery.

Operational Area, Operationsgebiet - field of operations, usually referring to West Berlin or West Germany.

NVA, Nationale Volksarmme – National People's Army, the GDR armed forces.

Operationsgebiet, OG, Operational Area – field of operations, usually referring to West Berlin or West Germany.

Petschaft – aluminium seal with unique numbers and coding, provided to persons with security clearance for sealing doors to offices and safes, using wax and thread.

Reichsbahn, Deutsche Reichsbahn, DR – GDR railways.

Sandmännchen, Unser Sandmännchen – Our Sandman, children's programme on East German television.

SED, Sozialistische Einheitspartei, the Party – GDR Communist party.

Sprelacart, Sprelakart – decorative laminate sheets, similar to Resopal and Formica.

Trabant – most widespread car in the GDR.

Transit train, Transitzug – train between West Germany and West Berlin, without passenger stops in the GDR (with the exception of Friedrichstraße). Cf.**Inter-zonal train**.

V100 – medium weight, general purpose diesel locomotive built in Hennigsdorf. Renumbered to Class 110.

Volkspolizei, Deutsche Volkspolizei, DVP – GDR police force.

W50 – medium sized diesel truck, ubiquitous in the GDR.

Wumme – gun.

Wofasept – disinfectant, used in practically every public building and train in the GDR.

Made in the USA
Las Vegas, NV
21 December 2021